Tales of Mexico and Spain

◇◇◇◇◇◇◇◇◇◇◇◇◇◇◇◇◇◇◇◇◇◇◇◇

Syd Love

Other Works by Syd Love

Novels
The Sundance Kid Died of Old Age in San Diego
Pancho Villa and the Loveliest Woman in Chihuahua
•

Translations
Legends of El Cid
(Romancero del Cid, authors unknown, a version
of *El Poema del Cid)*
Platero and I
(Platero y Yo, by Juan Ramón Jiménez)
Gypsy Storybook
(Romancero Gitano, by Federico García Lorca)
•

Essay
The Wisdom of Sancho Panza
•

Memoir
Time Gone By

Tales of Mexico and Spain

Published by
Journeys Press
200 K Street, Chula Vista, CA 91910

First Edition

ISBN: 978-0-9882643-6-6

Cover photos by the author: front, Mexican campesino statue, central plaza, Cuernavaca, Mexico, 2013, and El Cid Campeador, Vivar, Spain, 1967; rear, Hotel Delicias, Puerto Vallarta, Mexico, 1965, from a pastel drawing by Mario Gross of Montreal, Canada, and San Feliu de Llobregat, Spain

Cover and book design by Timothy W. Brittain (twbrit@cox.net)

To Maya

CONTENTS

TALES OF MEXICO

TALES OF SPAIN

COMPENDIUM

TALES OF MEXICO

THE BURRO

◇◇◇◇◇◇◇◇◇◇◇◇◇◇◇◇◇◇◇

Sunny Esperanza had hoped to always live in the friendly little town at the shore of the grand bay, had been born there and gone through all six grades there. She owned a reputation of being bright and ambitious. Sunny also enjoyed renown among family and peers for her skills in converting cotton cloth into purses, blouses, and dresses with exquisite embroidery, for weaving reeds into hats, and turning strips of leather and slabs of tire rubber into sandals and huaraches.

The Esperanza family lived in a small home of whitewashed bricks with a red tile roof, the bricks unevenly made, the tiles faded. With other humble dwellings it sat on the northerly outskirts of the community. The father, a fisherman, could walk to work. The mother took in sewing and washing.

When Mrs. Esperanza gave birth to their first daughter they named her after the Virgin of Guadalupe and grandmothers on both sides. But when they observed that they had an extraordinarily happy child who smiled and laughed continually they began calling her some English words her father had learned helping tourists fish: Sunshine, sometimes Sunny.

They had little income, but for Sunny's fifteenth birthday

they saved enough to make a fiesta, a *quinceañera* no participant could ever forget.

When Sunny met Julio Durante at her gala party she fell in love right in the middle of the mariachis' playing *Jarabe Tapatío*. In mere moments Julio had succumbed to Sunny's saucy smile, large brown eyes, and silken black hair flowing to the small of her back. Julio, seventeen, tall for his age, delighted her with chatter and attentiveness. They swore to marry after one year.

"You have a good job in your uncle's store," Sunny said, "and I can earn money with my sewing and handicrafts."

"In the store we can sell what you make. We can get a home of our own."

Sunny's parents opposed the young couple's plan.

"You know we want you to marry Tauro Pamposado," her father said.

"I don't like him."

"You've never met him. They say Tauro has extensive land holdings on the mountain."

"So what? Julio and I have made plans."

"Tauro's father and I were good friends," her father said. "We'll ask Tauro to visit."

"Don't ask him on my account."

"You'll like Tauro. Everyone says he's quite handsome and personable."

"So is Julio."

"Julio is just a boy. Tauro is older. He sold cars for a rich man in Guadalajara until recently when his father died. A mature man like that is ideal for you. Tauro will protect you and teach you so much." Her father paused, then added, "And he's said to be well off."

"But I don't want to live on the mountain. And there are bandits up there."

"You're thinking of Guerrero."

"And Indians," Sunny said.

"The Huichol and Nahua are tame," her mother interjected.

"Cougars and bears."

"They're up much higher," her father said.

"What if Mount Colima erupts?"

"It's nowhere near."

"Mama, help me . . ."

In the following week when Sunny met Tauro over coffee and churros at her home she agreed that he was handsome. He didn't seem old despite being nearly thirty, and he stood tall, displaying a mustache like Vicente Fernández grew. Tauro wore good black boots, jeans, a doeskin jacket, blue dress shirt, red string tie, and broad-brimmed black sombrero.

Sunny didn't notice that Julio frowned during her recounting of the meeting with Tauro, didn't seem at all enthusiastic. "My parents want me to marry him. Tauro knows Guadalajara and Mexico City too."

"What do you think?"

"Julio, don't be silly."

Two weeks passed before Tauro visited again. "I had to look after my land," he said, "and the governor needed to see me."

When Sunny exulted to Julio about meeting with Tauro a second time Julio's scowl extinguished her smile. She wondered about his lack of interest in her comments. *Jealous? But Julio is my boyfriend, not this Tauro.* "What's the matter, Julio? Is there trouble at the store?"

A week later a happy Sunny reported that Tauro invited her to see his rancho. "It's a three-hour walk, but he's going to rent horses for us. We'll be back before sunset."

"There's a Cantinflas movie tonight. I want to take you."

"Of course."

"If you're not too sore to sit some more."

Julio went alone to the movie.

The next day Sunny stopped by his uncle's store. She

walked with difficulty and grimaces. "Julio, I'm sorry about last night."

Julio nodded, rested his hands on the countertop.

"We spent too much time at his rancho. When we returned the horses Tauro suggested we have dinner at a restaurant he liked at Playa de Oro."

Julio nodded.

"I felt so hungry." She waited. "It had been such a long day." Sunny touched his hand. He pulled his hand away.

"I liked the food."

"That's nice." He looked past her to the street.

"We saw a beautiful sunset."

"So did I."

"Did you like the movie, Julio?"

"What do you think? Cantinflas."

"Tauro said he saw it in Guadalajara at the Cine—I forget."

"Doesn't matter."

Sunny caught his tone, saw his distress. *Must have eaten some bad shrimp last night.*

In the evening at dinner with her parents and siblings Sunny talked so much about the previous day she almost ignored her chicken enchiladas and beans topped with goat cheese.

"The trip up the mountain is rugged in places, but has lots of pines and mesquite, coconut palms and bananas and century plants. And Tauro showed me other trees I'd never seen, like chicle and the elephant ear. He has a small adobe house with a corrugated tin roof covered by palm fronds. The floor's hard-packed dirt, like here. The Río Cuale flows right through his land." She took a bite of enchilada, chewed for a moment, and continued.

"Corn and beans grow all over, and he has chickens and a burro. The next house is just a ten-minute walk. The people there, the Hurtados, take care of Tauro's place and his dog when he's away. They invited us to lunch." At sunset Sunny had thrilled to their bayside dinner and the view. "Tauro was so attentive I felt like an Azteca princess. We talked and talked. Tauro let me have a sip of wine from his glass."

Sunny Esperanza and Tauro Pamposado married three months later in a civil ceremony at the Palacio Municipal. He hired a man to carry Sunny's belongings in two cardboard boxes, and they walked up the mountain, though Sunny didn't like the idea of living in the house where Tauro's parents died.

"Couldn't we live somewhere else?"

"Why?" Tauro paid the man who toted Sunny's bundles and sent him down the trail. "I told you this would be our home. I represent the third generation of Pamposados to live here."

"I know, but now that I'm here it feels creepy."

"Are you seeing ghosts?" He laughed.

"It just doesn't feel comfortable, Tauro. And I miss the town."

"You'll get accustomed to this life."

While Tauro toiled in the fields of corn and beans Sunny sat at the kitchen table and made a work shirt for him. She made a housedress for herself and a bonnet to shade her face while outside.

"Tauro," Sunny said one day at lunch, "I wish I had a sewing machine."

"Did you see any power lines when I gave you a tour here?"

"There is one you work with your foot."

"You don't need it." Tauro scooted his chair back and walked outside to sit with his dog under the elephant ear tree. He also sat with a pint bottle of *raicilla*, a whiskey he made from the *cimarrón* maguey. Sunny watched him for a moment through the doorway before picking up the dishes and placing them into the sink. And she saw she didn't have any water. Sunny called through the doorway to her husband. "I'm out of water, Tauro. Please get me some."

"Can't you see I'm resting?"

Sunny stared at him, frowned at the dirty dishes, and picked up the bucket. "Never mind," she said when she passed Tauro at the tree.

"It's just a short walk." Tauro sipped from the bottle.

The dog, a large brown male without a name, followed Sunny to the stream, sat beside her while Sunny leaned over to fill the bucket, and accompanied her home.

In these first few weeks of marriage Sunny realized that Tauro did not possess lots of land like her father said, merely sharecropped a field on the slope. Sunny thought he didn't do much. He had little income. She noticed he rested frequently under the elephant ear tree, did so not only after eating. Sunny observed that Tauro had lost his attentiveness toward her. And she discovered that the bedroom lacked the thrills and excitement her older girlfriends had whispered to her amid their giggles. And she lived in boredom.

To occupy her time Sunny planted a small vegetable garden beside the house.

"Tauro," she said one day after breakfast, "even without a sewing machine I can make dresses and blouses and purses and embroider them. I'll use my own clothes to make patterns. It will be slow, but I can do it. And with all the reeds on the riverbank here I can make hats, even huaraches if we can find an old tire. And we can take them to the store of my friend Julio's uncle. Tourists like such items. The neighbor has some cloth she said I could start with."

"We carry it down the mountain?"

"Sure. A little bit every trip. It would be extra income for us."

"You do it." He walked outside and took his hoe into the cornfield.

When the next time came for Tauro to gather firewood he told Sunny to do that too.

"That's your job, Tauro."

"Not any longer."

"I don't know how to handle the burro."

"I'll show you."

Sunny scowled while Tauro instructed her how to secure the wooden rack to the little gray animal's back and loop the lead rope around its muzzle. *My father told me you would teach me things. Thank you so much.*

"She's smart." Tauro patted the burro's neck. "Once she knows where you're headed, if she's been there once or twice, you won't need to lead her or switch her rump either."

"Tauro, I'd rather not be in charge of gathering the firewood."

"You'll get used to it."

"I should have gloves to protect my hands."

"Why? I don't use gloves."

Tauro had not named the burro. Sunny called her Juana after a sturdy girlfriend who delivered bottled water in the town, though she handled only the smaller bottles. Sunny found the burro to be obedient, docile, sure footed and strong and willing. She looked forward to the day she would fill the burlap sacks on Juana's back with her own products to sell in the city instead of wood to burn in the cook stove. *At least Tauro cuts up or breaks the longer branches.*

"Tauro, if we had milk cans with lids, like I've seen in the town, the cans could ride on Juana's back. I could use a bucket to fill them, and she could carry water for me."

"You couldn't lift a milk can full of water off the burro."

"You could do that."

"No. My back is bothering me."

"Maybe you sit too much leaning against the elephant ear tree."

Tauro glared at her.

Sunny lowered her eyes. "I'm sorry."

"Don't talk to me like that again."

With pride of accomplishment and with enthusiasm about her skills Sunny examined the two stacks of embroidered blouses, dresses, and purses along with reed hats she had prepared for the store of Julio's uncle. She had placed everything onto the kitchen table for Tauro's approval.

When he entered, sweating and throwing his hat onto a chair, Tauro frowned at her work. "What's all this clutter?"

She told him.

"I need my lunch."

"I'll clear the table. Early tomorrow can we take everything down the mountain?"

"You can follow the trail downhill, can't you?"

"It's such a big trip, Tauro. I thought you'd like to—"

"My back, remember? But bring me some Cuban cigars and a liter of good tequila. I'm about out of *raicilla* and can't make any more right now."

After breakfast the next morning Tauro, complaining about his back, returned to bed. Sunny affixed the rack to Juana's back, hung burlap sacks to it, and filled the sacks with her products. She dreaded the long descent but looked forward to seeing Julio and her family.

The big brown dog accompanied Sunny and Juana. Sunny called him Compadre.

"This is exquisite work, Sunshine. So much beautiful embroidery, and by hand. My customers will love all this. And the tourist season is just starting."

"Thank you. If I had cloth I could bring more."

"I'll give you an advance. Bring all you can. Now you youngsters go for a walk while I take care of these items. You haven't seen each other for a while." Julio's uncle, Inocencio Durante, smiling and humming, began itemizing and tagging Sunny's work for display.

Outside the shop on busy Avenida Ignacio Vallarta, the magnificent bay a few steps away, Julio led the burro, and Sunny walked with him along the cobblestone street to the livery. "They won't charge much for this little animal. Did you have trouble controlling her?"

"My dog controlled her. I just followed." Compadre accompanied Sunny and Julio.

With Juana installed at the livery they walked to the central plaza, where Julio purchased ice cream cones and they sat on a wrought-iron bench under the orange-and-scarlet blooms of a royal poinciana. They could see the bay, the passersby, and the bandstand.

Julio hadn't spoken since ordering the ice cream.

"So," Sunny said, "how have you been?"

"Fine. You?"

"Fine."

They watched the bay, the idlers, the bandstand.

"Have any good movies come to town?"

"Some. Old ones. You know."

"Dolores del Río? María Félix?"

"Both."

"They're so pretty."

"So are you, Sunny."

She let Compadre finish her ice cream. *Please don't ask me too many questions. I don't know what to say.* "I miss living here. The bay, the movies . . . certain people."

Julio finished his ice cream, watched the bay.

"Sometimes I take a chair and sit under a big madrone and sew. Do you know the madrone has smooth red bark?"

Julio studied the pelicans and sea gulls and terns over the bay.

"I need an old tire to make soles for huaraches."

"You also need leather and an awl and the right kind of knife and twine. Forget huaraches. The items you made are excellent. Uncle will sell them easily. Stick with those."

Julio had not said so much all afternoon. Sunny liked the authority in his voice.

"I'd better get back." Julio stood.

"Walk me to my parents' home?"

Julio, unspeaking, accompanied Sunny and Compadre.

Smiling, Sunny thanked him and offered her hand. *My dog talks more than you do.* "I'd like to stop by the store tomorrow to purchase cloth and thread."

"Someone will be there."

"'Someone'?"

Sunny enjoyed being with her family again, relished the carne asada, and loved sleeping in her former bed.

"Is it cold at night up there?"

"We're not up so high, Mama."

"Are the neighbors friendly?"

"I met one couple. They were all right."

"Is Tauro good to you?"

"He gets gruff sometimes. I don't know what I do wrong." *Too many questions.*

"You don't smile and laugh like before."

"I'm fine, Mama."

She hurried to Inocencio Durante's store immediately after a breakfast of eggs, chorizo, milk, coffee, corn tortillas, and beans. Compadre had received a tin dish filled with scraps.

"You've been kind, Mr. Durante. And nice to see you again, Julio."

Julio nodded.

"You just take that cloth you purchased," Inocencio told her, "and turn it into more of those wonderful dresses, blouses, and purses like you brought yesterday."

"I'm not sure when I can return with more."

"It doesn't matter. One of us will be here. Julio can run the store as well as I can."

Julio helped Sunny carry the material. On the way to the livery she stopped. "Almost forgot. I need to get a bottle of tequila and some Cuban cigars."

"For him, I suppose."

Sunny felt Julio's tone slice into her, a machete slashing through a banana frond. *I should have made the purchases earlier for Tauro.* She bit her lip, decided on a saucy counterattack. "They're for me. On the mountain we don't have movies for entertainment."

Julio led her to a store and stood outside while she made the purchases. At the livery he helped her load the burro and told her good-bye. "Go easy on the cigars until you get used to them."

Sunny gave her head an impudent turn and started off with Juana and Compadre.

Halfway up the trail she tugged on the rope. Juana stopped, turned her head, and looked at Sunny, who sat on a large rock under a mesquite. Compadre sat beside her, and Juana nibbled on grass while Sunny rested and reminisced. *Julio pretended he didn't enjoy seeing me, but I know different. I guess he hasn't become accustomed to me being married to Tauro. I know he's hurt. But he'll soon get over the feelings he had for me, just I have forgotten my feelings for him. We were just kids. He'll be busy in the store and won't have time to think about me. But I'm so glad I got to visit with him a little, to see my family and the town again.*

She rested once more before arriving, proud of her successful trip and eager to show Tauro her cash advance, the first money she'd ever earned other than for cleaning hotel rooms.

"Did you remember my cigars? Where are they?"

"In one of the sacks, Tauro."

"And my tequila?"

"With the cigars."

Tauro had dropped his hoe and cut across the bean field to intercept her, scatterng the chickens and meeting Sunny at the front door. "Which sack? Hurry."

"The one closest to you, I believe."

Tauro opened the sack and dug into it.

"You've been in the field. Don't dirty my new material."

He stopped and glared at her.

"Please?"

With Tauro on her heels Sunny carried the sacks into the house and unloaded the contents onto the table. Tauro grabbed the cigars with one hand, the tequila with the other.

"This is not one of the good tequilas." He extended the bottle toward her.

"I'm not familiar with the liquors, Tauro."

"Next time get the best. Ask the clerk."

"Yes, Tauro." *I'll start out as soon as I feed the burro and the dog, prepare your meal, do your laundry, and mend your socks.* "Julio's uncle liked the clothes and purses I took to him."

Tauro finished unwrapping a cigar.

"Do you like what I selected to work on now?"

He glanced at the materials. "All right, I suppose." He started toward the door, stopped, and turned back. "How did you pay for that stuff? It better not be on credit."

Sunny explained about the advance Inocencio Durante gave her.

"So if your work doesn't sell I'm going to have to repay the advance?"

"Mr. Durante said it would sell." *So did Julio.*

"Is any of the advance left?"

Sunny reached into her blouse pocket and withdrew several bills to show him.

Tauro stepped up to her, snatched the money, and walked outside.

Compadre jumped out of his path. The chickens scattered.

First Sunny gave the neighbor, Celia Hurtado, cloth to replace what Celia had lent her. Next, again using her own clothing as patterns she often varied, Sunny cut cloth, sewed, and embroidered all day every day. She took breaks only to fix meals and sometimes walk to the Hurtado home nearby to obtain garlic or another condiment she lacked, for her garden had not begun producing. Sunny liked Celia, pretty, in her mid-twenties, but loathed her husband, much older, slovenly, surly. She wondered why Celia didn't run away.

When Celia for the first time invited Sunny to stay for coffee and a chat, they had talked for only a few minutes when Tauro interrupted them. "You get home right now."

Without comment she obeyed. Compadre led the way.

In her kitchen, however, while Tauro watched from his chair, Sunny paused with hands in the tortilla dough and addressed him. "You didn't have to be rude."

Tauro stood and slapped her.

Sunny grabbed the sink to keep from falling, turned to see Tauro step outside, her glare at his back fatal had it been a dagger. She vowed to herself to never again stay to chat with Celia.

When Sunny had created enough blouses, dresses, purses, and hats for a load to take down the trail, she concocted two small birdcages from spines of palm fronds. *They*

don't weigh much so Juana won't mind. One on each side will
make her proud, like she has a heavy burden.

That night in bed she told Tauro. "I'd like to go into
town tomorrow after breakfast."

"If you're paid anything for that other work don't waste
it. And bring me more Cuban cigars and a bottle of tequila.
Ask the clerk like I told you."

"You're finished with that first bottle already?"

"Are you judging me?"

Sunny tensed. "I don't mean to."

"Good. Because we have something important to do."
He touched her breast.

She shivered with dread.

For most of the trek downhill Sunny wondered if the tourists had purchased any of the items she left at the store and,
if so, how many. And how much money would be hers? And
if no one bought anything she'd left, how much time would
she have to repay the advance? For the first time Sunny had
to consider such problems.

She also fretted about how different Tauro had become
toward her. *Does he not love me anymore? What do I do to*
make him that way? And do I love him the way I should? Cer-
tainly not today with my face puffed up and my jaw sore from
that slap. And the business in bed . . .

Sunny shrugged off the troubles with Tauro and continued following Juana and Compadre down the slope, looked
forward to being with her family, the food, the camaraderie,
the good bed. When Julio Durante seemed to burst into
her thoughts she realized Julio had hovered on the fringe all
along, watching, waiting. *Maybe he'll talk this time.*

Near the end of the three-hour descent, with thoughts
focused on reaching the store and on her being a business-
woman instead of a muleteer, Sunny watched the skyline for

the church tower, housetops, and the bay. She neglected her footing, twisted her ankle, and fell.

Sunny sat for a moment, caught her breath, and rubbed her ankle. She stood cautiously, looked down the trail and saw the dog and burro far ahead. "Compadre," she called.

The dog stopped, turned to watch her.

"Here, Compadre. Come."

The dog loped up to her, received a pat, and stood looking at her.

"I wish I could lean on you like a crutch, big boy. But I think I can make it. Go get Juana." She pointed down the slope. "Stop Juana. Stop her."

To Sunny's surprise and pleasure Compadre galloped toward the burro while Sunny limped after both. Compadre headed off the burro and tried to turn her back up the trail. "That's good enough, Compadre. It's all right." Sunny caught up with them. "Just go slow."

Sunny didn't realize until they reached the store that she had not flicked Juana with the switch nor given Compadre instructions except after her tumble.

"They didn't need me at all," she told Julio and his uncle.

"I bet they could lead you back up too," Inocencio Durante said. "I've seen animals that smart. Don't you agree, Julio?"

Julio nodded. "I'll unload the burro." He went outside where the animals waited.

"Young lady," Inocencio said, "I have lots of good news for you." He pulled a ledger from under the counter and opened it "This will take just a few minutes because I've kept a running total. Why don't you have a seat?"

"I'm too nervous." She limped outside to help Julio with the birdcages and two burlap sacks of blouses and dresses, purses and hats.

"I can handle it," Julio told her.

"It's nice to see you."

Julio mumbled something she missed and handed her the birdcages.

"I thought of making the cages at the last minute. I hope that's all right."

"They'll sell easily."

"How have you been?"

"Fine."

"It's nice to see you."

"You said that." Julio removed a sack from the burro, walked around the animal, and with one hand tried to untie the other sack.

Sunny set the cages onto the street, bumped him out of the way with her hip, and untied the sack. She carried it with one hand, the cages with the other, and preceded Julio inside. They set the sacks and cages onto a countertop.

"You're limping," Julio said.

"I tripped and fell."

"On your face?"

Sunny touched her swollen cheek. "Some. I'm all right."

"Sunny, look at this." Inocencio waved a piece of paper for her to see.

Sunny wished Julio's uncle had not interrupted them. *So it takes a pratfall like Charlie Chaplin to get Julio to say something personal. What should I do next time?*

"You see?" Inocencio pointed to a list and column of figures. "These are the items you made and the order I sold them in. On the right is the amount I received for each. I have only a blouse left. You brought more just in time. Business is very good. Tourists are all over the place like pelicans diving on a school of anchovies. Here's the gross total. See? Now I subtract the advance I gave you and take 40% for the store. I hope you find that fair."

Sunny's smile flashed. Her ponytail bounced.

Julio told her, "From other seamstresses Uncle takes half."

"And here's what you get. Your profit." Inocencio pointed to the bottom figure.

Sunny thrilled at the amount.

"I want you to bring more as fast that little burro can walk." He smiled.

"I'll do the best I can. I mean Juana and I."

"You have an assistant?"

"Juana is her burro," Julio said.

Inocencio laughed. "Got me. Anyway, I'm going to Guadalajara soon. I hear there's a store selling huge papier-mâché animals, like horses, bulls, dogs, giraffes. A famous artist from Mexico City makes them. If I like them I'll add a second story to display them. But whenever I go, my dear, you keep delivering. Julio will be here if I'm not."

Sunny purchased cloth, thread, and ribbons red, green, and white. Julio walked with her, carried everything to her family home while she tested two questions and received two grunts.

The swelling in her face had subsided, so no one in the family learned about Tauro's slap. After a large meal with her parents and siblings Sunny, accompanied by Compadre, went shopping. For herself she purchased a comb and brush, skin lotion and underwear. For Tauro she bought a box of Romeo and Julieta cigars and a liter of tequila whose blue-and-green label featured a horseshoe. The clerk recommended it as the best.

The next day following an early breakfast Sunny retrieved Juana from the livery, and her father loaded the burro with Sunny's purchases.

"Do you like life on the mountain?"

"Some things," Sunny said. "Like when I need plantains to fry I borrow Tauro's machete if he's not using it, and in two minutes I cut all I want. Reeds for the hats grow on the riverbank nearby. I made a vegetable patch. Birds and squirrels are all over."

"It's lush country. What do you do about meat?"

"We have chickens. The neighbors raise pigs."

"You don't laugh and smile as much as you used to."

She shrugged.

"How's Tauro doing?"

"His back bothers him. So do I."

"What are you talking about?"

"I can't seem to please him. I don't know what I do wrong." *I feel like a burro.*

"That sounds like something you should talk to your mother about."

"I'll try." *But I can't mention the time he slapped me. I'm too ashamed.*

"The thing about marriage, Sunny, is you have to work at it. I'm sure Tauro is just like my friend, his father, a good man. You do what he says and everything will be fine. Now you have your mother tape that ankle real tight. Are you sure you'll be all right?"

"I hardly feel it."

"I'm off to hunt fish. Come again soon." They hugged. He kissed her cheek.

She watched her father walk toward the pier. *Sometimes I wish you'd never brought Tauro into my life.*

Sunny stiffened when she saw Tauro's pleasure at seeing the cigars and tequila turn to wrath upon his noting the items she'd purchased for herself. "You already have a comb and brush. Take these back. And what do you need ribbons for on the mountain?"

"They're not for me, Tauro. I'll create bows and sew them on dresses or cut them to length and send them along as hair ribbons."

Tauro swept the items onto the floor.

Sunny sobbed. "Sometimes I hate you."

He knocked her down with a blow to her chest, kicked her in the ribs, jammed the cigars into his shirt pocket, and grabbed his bottle. "Don't ever speak to me like that again." Tauro walked outside, met Compadre growling at him, kicked at the dog, and missed.

Sunny, too angry and upset to cry, sat up slowly, gasped, and touched her side. When she stood she couldn't inhale deeply because pain stabbed her. But she collected her purchases from the dirt, took them into the bedroom, and collapsed on the bed. She lay there a long time.

For several days the pain prevented her from inhaling deeply, and she lowered her eyes if Tauro walked near. When he questioned her about doing that she apologized and thereafter remembered to look at him when he stood close. And she wondered not whether she loved Tauro the way a wife should but if she hated him the way a prisoner would.

One day when she sat sewing under the great madrone with its smooth red bark, Tauro on his way in from the fields stopped in front of her. He bent forward, scowling, legs spread. Sunny smelled the whiskey, saw his anger, wondered what she had done wrong. Compadre, dozing at her feet, got up and moved several paces away, sat, and watched Tauro.

"Why are you so slow, so listless, lately?"

Sunny stiffened, inhaled deeply, exhaled. "I might be catching a cold."

"And at night you go to bed early. I try to wake you and you say you're too tired."

"I can't help it. I am."

"How are you going to give me a son if you're so tired every night?"

"I'm sorry, Tauro." *He's drunk, must have a bottle hidden in the field. Be careful.*

"Is that all you have to say, you're 'sorry'?"

Sunny examined the sewing in her lap.

"Look at me when I talk to you."

She looked at him. *I hate you.* Her hands trembled.

Tauro spun about and staggered toward the house.

Compadre returned to his spot at her feet.

When Sunny awoke the next morning she felt ill. But she fixed breakfast and returned to her sewing as soon as Tauro headed for the fields. And she thought about Tauro's anger, his harshness, and sometimes his fury. *I keep trying to figure out what I do wrong, and I'm beginning to think it might not be me. He just seems to "aggravate" all by himself. And I can't love him when he's like this.* She sighed and continued sewing. *I'm not sure I can ever love him like I did at first—or thought I did.*

Her cold had gained on her by nightfall, and Sunny felt even worse the next morning. She knew that Julio and his uncle expected her with her handmade goods, and she had enough items to fill the two burlap bags. But she didn't feel strong enough to make the trip.

"Tauro," she said that evening at supper, "I'd like to send a shipment to the store."

"What do you mean 'send'? You're not thinking of sending it with me."

"Of course not. Juana and Compadre know the way. I'll put in a note for Mr. Durante and Julio. They can hold my payment until I get rid of this cold, and I'll include what I need in material and thread. That same day they send Juana and Compadre back up the trail with it."

"Maybe I should go after all and collect the money."

"Certainly, if you wish."

"It's too much trouble." Tauro used a tortilla to scoop up the last of his beans. "Do it your way. But they better not cheat you. And if anything happens to my burro you'll pay dearly."

Sunny sipped water from her ceramic mug.

"Did you hear me? And I need more tequila and cigars."

"Yes, Tauro."

Early the next morning Sunny asked Tauro to load the burro.

"You do it," he said.

By the time she loaded Juana and led her and Compadre down the trail a short distance, so they would understand their duty, Sunny felt so weak she had to sit on the ground to rest in the shade of a pine. When she felt strong enough she returned to the house and spent the rest of the day in bed except for making Tauro a midday meal and washing his soiled underwear.

The sky had begun to darken when Sunny awoke to a large brown dog's muzzle resting on her hand. "Hi, Compadre." She patted his head, felt like kissing him, and began to muster the strength to unload Juana and feed both animals. They knew to go to the stream for water.

Tauro arrived from the fields just as Sunny finished taking in the supplies Inocencio Durante sent. "Where are my cigars and tequila?"

Sunny trembled, feared she might collapse. "I'm sorry. I forgot to ask Mr. Durante or Julio to include them." *If he knocks me down I'm going to grab the butcher knife when I get up.*

Tauro swore at her, glared at her.

Sunny, knees weak, hands shaking, showed Tauro a sheet of paper with an accounting. "It's more than last time."

Tauro examined the paper. "Lot of good it does. The money's there, not here."

"We don't have anything to spend it on here anyway." *Uh-oh. Did I say the wrong thing?*

Tauro swore again, scowled at the paper, at Sunny, and walked outside.

Sunny watched, hoped he wouldn't kick Compadre, saw the dog hurry out of Tauro's way. She exhaled, hadn't realized she'd held her breath, and returned to the bed, where she removed from her dress pocket the personal note Julio had included:

Julio hoped she would recover soon. He missed seeing her. Uncle would leave next week for Guadalajara. Maybe next time they could have ice cream at the plaza again. Send more hats.

Sunny fell asleep with hope and fear fighting like Azteca and conquistador for position in her tears.

Thinking of Julio and rereading his note gave Sunny strength to fix Tauro's meals, feed the animals, and fetch water. Within two days she felt strong enough to sew for brief periods and tend to her vegetable garden. But she couldn't push aside the hopelessness of her existence, felt it would scar her hands, round her shoulders, bend her back, and sag her belly. She often cried, though never in Tauro's presence. He usually worked on the far side of the fields, and his being out of sight and sound pleased her.

When Sunny again felt at full strength she concentrated on sewing enough for another delivery to be sold at the Durante store, which she thought of as Julio's.

Soon she decided to rest from sewing. The midmorning sun glowed warmly on the fields, but elsewhere the palms, pines, firs, and other trees provided shade. Sunny picked up a burlap sack to hold the long skinny leaves she would strip from palm fronds to weave into hats to top off the next load. *They're closer than the reeds at the stream and serve just as well.* She took her butcher knife and started out when she noted Tauro's machete leaning against the wall near the door. *Better than the knife. I'll borrow it.*

"Come on, Compadre." Wagging his tail, Compadre rose from the base of the madrone, where he always accompanied Sunny when she sat there and sewed.

Sunny walked off the trail to a spot where, like a family, palms clustered halfway to the neighboring home. With the machete she slashed through several fronds and stripped the leaves. *I'll just cut a few. That way they will hardly be missed.*

When Compadre growled softly, the hair on the back of his neck raised like tines on a wire brush. Sunny paused and listened, looked in the same direction Compadre did. She heard someone moving about. Next came a man's light laughter, then a woman's. She detected more movement, a man's laugh slightly stronger than before, a woman's giggle, low conversation.

The man's voice belonged to Tauro.

Sunny patted Compadre, whispered, "Be quiet. Let's go see." She wove her way through a cluster of banana trees, Compadre following. When she neared the end of the stand she stopped and peeked through them to an open spot at the edge of the cornfield. And Sunny saw Tauro, standing with his back to her, pull up his pants and fasten his belt. When he sat to put on his shoes Sunny could see the woman better: her neighbor, Celia Hurtado, slipping her dress on over her head, then sitting to put on sandals. Celia giggled. Tauro laughed.

Compadre growled softly.

Sunny patted him, sobbed, but stifled the next sob before it could be heard, before it tore into her heart. "Come, Compadre." She led him back to the sack of palm leaves she'd stripped from their spines, and she sat and cried softly. She didn't know what to do, couldn't think clearly. *If I confront him he might kill me.* She lifted the sack of cuttings, picked up the machete, choked off her sobs. "Let's go home, Compadre."

Walking through the bananas and into the oaks and pines and firs, they neared the main trail when Sunny heard someone moving through the forest at an angle to her, a person perhaps heading for the same path. *Oh. That might be*

Tauro. She paused. *I'll let him reach the trail first. At home I'll pretend I didn't see them. But how can I live with what I know? I hate him so.*

And Tauro arrived a few feet in front of her, faced her, glared.

Sunny gasped. She dropped the bag.

Compadre moved several yards away, sat growling.

"What have you been up to?" Tauro looked around. "Who gave you permission to use my machete?" He stepped forward, reaching. "I'll take that."

Sunny backed away. "I only cut a few palm fronds."

Tauro stepped close, grabbed her arm that held the long, heavy knife.

"Please don't hurt me, Tauro."

"You've been spying on me." He punched her in the forehead, knocking her onto her back, and she dropped the machete. On his knees Tauro straddled Sunny and began choking her.

Compadre growled louder, leaped at Tauro, clamping his jaws around Tauro's forearm.

Tauro yelled, stood, and tried to dislodge the dog.

Sunny sat up, grabbed the machete, and slashed Tauro's nearest leg.

Still trying to pry Compadre off his arm, Tauro cried out and fell to his knees.

Sunny screamed. Using both hands she swung the machete into Tauro's neck and watched his head loll onto his shoulder, blood gushing.

Julio Durante, managing the store during his uncle's absence in Guadalajara, enjoyed seeing the little burro and the large brown dog arrive along the cobblestone street and stop in front of the store. He wished he also would be greeting

Sunny, but maybe next time she would accompany the animals. At least there should be a note.

He stepped outside, gave Compadre several welcoming pats, and set out a pan of water for him. He rubbed Juana's neck, promised to unload her as soon as he read the note from Sunny.

Good Lord, Julio thought when he saw what lay beneath the note. *Sunny! My God. Jesús, María, and José. I know you're strong willed, but this . . .* He started reading:

"Dear Julio: Tauro had a horrible accident. I don't go with the animals this time, just in case someone I might meet along the trail gets curious. It would be too difficult to explain this to strangers, and I can't believe it happened, but I can tell you everything when I see you, which will be soon. Dearest Julio, please find a way to get rid of Tauro's segments. I wrapped them in some of his clothes so blood wouldn't drip on the trail. When you send the animals back I will load Juana with my sewing, my personal belongings, and accompany them down the mountain to you. And I will never go up again. I hope you can accept me, also my burro and dog."

Julio, hands trembling, unfastened the burlap bags from the burro's back and toted them into the store. He carried them one at a time because of their weight, not like when their loads had been clothes and hats. *I hope she means what she says about coming back for keeps.*

He closed and locked the front door, lowered the blinds on door and windows, caught his breath. Julio leaned against a counter and crossed his arms, examined the well-packed burlap bags on the floor. His stomach convulsed. *This is gruesome. Sunny, what have you done? Quickest would be wait until dark and stuff the bags into the trash cans in the alley and drag them to the rear of someone else's property. But someone might hear the racket and see me.*

Julio, astounded by Sunny's shipment, concerned about her, walked around to examine the floor's paving stones. The unevenness of some became evident for the first time even though Julio had walked on them since before he could remember. He stopped and nodded. *Sure. I'll pry up several pavers, dig a hole, deposit the bags, throw in some dirt, and put the pavers back.*

He walked to the rear and returned with a crowbar. *But Tauro's segments would settle. There would be a low spot.*

Julio thought for a few moments, nodded, and started removing all the pavers. With renewed enthusiasm Julio dug a deep hole, spread Tauro's parts evenly throughout the excavation, and covered them with soil, pavers, and rocks from the edge of the street. *Pack it tight. Scatter leftover soil in the alley.* Tomorrow he would round up some workers and frame the burial site with wood, add cross supports, cover them with planks, and pour a concrete floor. *I'll put a good indoor-outdoor carpet over it. Uncle will be pleased.*

Tauro's disappearance surprised and disappointed Sunny's parents. But when she told them how he had beaten her they welcomed her back home. Her father threatened to hunt Tauro down and horsewhip him, but Sunny assured them Tauro had left the mountain for keeps.

"He won't ever be back," Sunny said. "We can sell Juana, but I'd like to keep Compadre."

Her parents and siblings embraced the canine addition to the family.

Within two months workers had completed a second story to his shop, and Inocencio Durante installed Sunny upstairs in a corner window with view of the bay, an electric sewing machine, and freedom to create blouses and dresses to sell, sun hats and purses and rebozos.

Large papier-mâché animals roamed the room.

Compadre spent each day at her feet.

The little shop thrived as never before.

Julio climbed the stairs so often to chat with Sunny that his uncle scolded him.

Everyone said that as a couple Sunny and Julio sparkled like the stars at night.

And they agreed that Sunshine Esperanza smiled and laughed the way she had before she went up the mountain.

The Patriarch

Only two people knew that the elderly Gregorio Santana was two years older than UItiminio Huerta. Those two were Gregorio and Ultiminio themselves. But because of an insidious plan Ultiminio concocted when they were much younger, everyone else in the mountain village of San Luis thought Ultiminio the elder. The way this came about exemplified the luck and cunning that characterized him for many years.

Gregorio learned of the scheme when Ultiminio gave himself an extravagant party in observance of what he announced as his seventy-fifth birthday. Offerings included barbecued shoat, beans, roasted ears of corn, tortillas of wheat and corn, jalapeños, mountain chiles for the daring, and plenty of pulque and homemade whiskey, which in San Luis they called *raicilla*.

Residents along with visitors from nearby villages jammed the San Luis town square. A mariachi trio Ultiminio imported from a larger community played continually, and children escaped inhibiting eyes of adults to kick soccer balls in the side streets, climb trees, and ride burros in the mayor's corral. Ultiminio, smile beaming as brightly as the midsummer sun, accepted congratulations and thanks throughout the day.

"Something is wrong here," Gregorio told his nephew, Isidro Acosta. "As far back as I can remember, Ultiminio has been two years younger than me. Now he is one year older."

"How can that be?"

"I also would like an answer to that."

They sat in hide-covered bucket chairs and sipped pulque in the shade of the cantina overhang. They enjoyed the music from the mariachis, watched couples dancing in the hard-packed dirt street, and inhaled the piquant aromas of beans and barbecue and corn tortillas.

"And another thing," Gregorio said. "Why does he think he's some tycoon who can arrange a fiesta and even hire musicians? He's not the governor of Jalisco nor the mayor of Puerto Vallarta." Gregorio pounded his chair arm and spat. "Ultiminio is not even our patriarch."

"Calm yourself." Isidro touched his uncle's shoulder. "My mother says you and he have quarreled forever. You know how he is. Every time I visit here you rant about him like a fisherman who lost the big one to a shark."

"I have always tolerated his bragging and arrogance."

"Sometimes."

"But not this." Gregorio pounded his chair arm again, took a deep breath, exhaled. "Do you remember the time he . . ." And Gregorio expelled a lengthy enumeration of what he called Ultiminio's black deeds.

"I witnessed a couple of those incidents, Uncle. But, remember, I'm much younger than you and don't get up here often from the city."

"Good fortune for you that you haven't known him for so long."

"Have more pulque and relax."

When the mariachis took a break Ultiminio climbed onto the tribune and picked up the megaphone. He thanked everyone for attending, reminded them to eat and drink heartily, and called on the village patriarch, Eustaquio Aguilar, to address the gathering.

"There he goes again," Gregorio said. "I hope Don Eustaquio refuses."

"He will. This morning I heard him tell people in the general store that he felt poorly. He purchased a bottle of aspirin and some herbs."

Gregorio looked toward a corner of the town square, where he spotted Eustaquio sitting on a wooden bench under a royal poinciana. Eustaquio wore boots, well-worn black suit, and black sombrero edged by silver embroidery and with silver conchos around the crown. Many of his great-grandchildren clustered near. "You're right. He's motioning refusal."

Ultiminio resumed talking of his glorious birthday celebration, and someone interrupted. Gregorio couldn't hear the man's question, but Ultiminio's reply explained it.

"I am glad you asked, my friend. My wife had the same question earlier today, and others of you, older friends, have asked me privately. After all, we are a small community. No one has any secrets." He paused and smiled.

Gregorio thought Ultiminio's chest expanded.

"You see, friends, long ago when I was around twenty I started thinking about growing old. And I didn't like the idea. So I chopped three years off my age. Thereafter if anyone happened to inquire I gave them the lesser number. But lately I like the idea of growing old. "To be elderly is to have dignity, to exhibit wisdom, to be interesting. I am now proud of my age. So today I am announcing my true age of seventy-five. I'm sure you understand."

Jesús, María, and José. Gregorio spat. "Well, so what? Why should anyone care?" He thought a moment and realized why someone might care: "He wants to be our patriarch."

"The oldest?"

"Exactly."

"He'll have to wait a long time."

"He might. And he and I are already among the oldest."

"That's such a far-away time, Uncle. Who knows who will replace Don Eustaquio? Besides, is that such a grand thing?"

"Indeed it is. To be patriarch, the oldest man in the village, is the most exalted and coveted achievement that can be realized in a mountain community like San Luis. Every Independence Day he gets to give The Shout of Dolores. He leads the Posadas at Christmas, and he burns the Judas effigy on Good Friday. In short the patriarch is our most-honored personage at all festivities of religious or athletic character."

"Like being mayor?" Isidro said.

"Much better because the mayor has to handle politics. Being patriarch means that children undertake errands for him more enthusiastically than for other adults. It means the men seek his counsel about crops even though they have sown the same crops and raised them the same way for generations.

"These same men seek his wisdom about possible mates, at first for themselves, later for their sons and daughters. And if the patriarch is without a wife, the women of the village prepare his meals and do his washing and mending and housework."

"Don't tell me he gets to change the weather."

Gregorio laughed.

They watched the crowd and enjoyed the music throughout the afternoon. Gregorio suppressed his antipathy toward Ultiminio, and Isidro told the latest news about the small city where he lived at the rim of the bay.

The fiesta lasted until after dark. Several fights broke out, but no one suffered a serious injury because none of the participants carried machete or knife.

Early the next day at the plaza, with scarlet-and-orange poinciana blooms coloring the background, Gregorio thanked his nephew for visiting and for the reading material he'd brought. They shook hands and embraced, shook hands again.

"Give your mother my love."

"Of course, Uncle." Isidro thanked Gregorio for his hospitality and stationed himself on a bench of the open-sided jungle bus that would carry him down the mountain and home.

When they were boys, Gregorio shy and awkward, Ultiminio gregarious and athletic, argued over who would be first to dive from the rock into the river. Ultiminio always defeated Gregorio in foot races and arm wrestling. They quarreled during their marble games and soccer matches. They fought over girlfriends and later over women, disagreed on the best way to make *raicilla* from the *cimarrón* maguey, and contested the drinking of it.

Ultiminio stood taller than Gregorio, and Gregorio realized that everyone considered his competitor much the handsomer. In their youth Ultiminio had been the ablest horseman in the village and better than anyone leaning from the saddle of his racing mount and jerking from the sand the rooster buried to its neck. He could throw a lariat and play the guitar and sing. He grew a larger, plusher mustache than Gregorio's.

The villagers knew Ultiminio to be wily and to embellish his stories, but they generally liked him, or tolerated him, and most had learned not to loan him money. Because of his loquaciousness, four times they had elected him their delegate to the nearby town and twice named him their representative to the district landowners' association. Ultiminio never missed an opportunity to mention that he was a man of action.

"I have seen Guadalajara twice," he frequently said. "But Gregorio, he stays home with those books and magazines the jungle bus brings him."

The villagers of San Luis knew Gregorio for his humility, uprightness, loyalty to friends, his reading skills, and tenacity at work in his fields. His fine string of burros, which hauled firewood and crops and could be ridden, owned the reputation of infallibly footed and stronger and more obedient that anyone else's. He readily lent them to other men.

When the pox assaulted San Luis the disease nicked Gregorio's face permanently. Ultiminio remained unmarked.

Ultiminio married the prettiest girl in San Luis. Everyone feted them, though Gregorio stood at the rear of the festivities. They created two strong sons and four attractive daughters.

Gregorio never married. Instead he descended the mountain on the jungle bus once a month and went to the women in one of the brothels in the small city at the shore of the bay.

After Gregorio twisted an ankle and couldn't work for three days Ultiminio never consoled him. When Ultiminio suffered a week-long illness Gregorio visited twice.

In his quiet way Gregorio enjoyed more friendships than Ultiminio did. But one by one the older residents died. One day Gregorio realized that he and Ultiminio were the oldest men except for Don Eustaquio. Ultiminio's lie about his age began to oppress Gregorio. If he outlived Ultiminio, Gregorio should become the patriarch when Don Eustaquio died. And he yearned for that honor. Ultiminio's vile deception stood in his way. *I'll talk to Ultiminio. He should correct his lie.*

Don Eustaquio was ninety-six, Gregorio eighty-two, and Ultiminio claimed eighty-three on that warm summer day when he asked to rent Gregorio's burros, which Gregorio maintained out of loyalty and kindness even though he had recently retired.

"I don't accept rent for them from friends," Gregorio said, "only from strangers. You know that. Everyone does." He sat in a bucket chair in front of his small home of adobe with a tin roof covered by palm fronds.

"You are saying I'm a friend?"

"Not like you could be."

"I prefer to pay you." He leaned against a post supporting Gregorio's roof overhang.

"No pay. How many do you need?"

"Kind of you. All four."

"You must have quite a project." Gregorio began making a cigarette.

"The mayor wants to cover our main street with cobblestones."

"I hadn't heard. You mean to haul rocks."

"Yes."

"I can let you use only two. My others are too old."

"But with your four and my two, my sons and I can bring the rocks in fewer trips."

Gregorio lighted his cigarette, inhaled, blew smoke. "My old ones lead the string but could not do what you want." *Maybe this is the time to talk about his lie, put pressure on him.*

"I get a bonus if I finish the job quickly. I could give you some of my bonus."

"I don't need money from anyone named Ultiminio Huerta." *I bet he knows why I'm talking to him so sternly.*

Ultiminio spread his arms wide. "I know we've had our little disagreements in times past. But that had all been in fun."

"Don't you think you're too old to haul rocks and build streets on your hands and knees?" *That should show him my line of thinking.*

"I have two sons to do most of the work. All I need is your fine burros."

"Only two."

"What about this, Gregorio: I won't load the two older ones heavily."

"I think you should borrow someone else's."

"The rocks are most abundant upriver. Then we have to descend with the loads. Your burros can handle a trail better than any. Everyone knows that."

Gregorio looked at the cornfield on the slope, studied the clouds formed like a snow-covered Sierra Madre, watched children playing in front of the little adobe church across the street. And he examined Ultiminio's face. *Right here in front of the church is the place to confront him. Too bad the padre won't pass this way again for two weeks. But I'll call out to the children to bring some parents to be witnesses.* "I lend you the four on two conditions: You load the two older burros with only half the weight you place on the others, and you recant the fantastic lie you told at your birthday celebration a few years ago."

"What lie?"

"About your age."

"But that's the truth, Gregorio. I am a year older than you."

"You are not."

"Your memory has failed. Ask my wife. She knows I had subtracted three years."

"She can know only what you told her. She came later from a different village."

"Ask Don Eustaquio."

"Everyone knows his memory can't be trusted."

"I'll give you my entire bonus."

"I don't want your bonus. I want the truth in front of witnesses."

"But I'm telling the truth."

Ultiminio's insistence on maintaining his prevarication angered Gregorio. He looked at the church again, noted how the clouds above the cornfield had enlarged and darkened, felt the breeze, smelled rain in the air. *Is my memory wrong? I don't think so. But what can I do? I can't squeeze it out of him, and certainly I can't spread the word myself. How greedy and contrived would that seem? Maybe this is not the time. I always lend my burros to our people. If I don't accommodate Ultiminio the village will think I've become selfish.* "What about the other condition?"

"Of course. Only half as much weight as on the others."

"Don't forget."

"I'll take excellent care of them."

"And we'll continue this conversation about your age another time."

The rain soon arrived, tentative at first, then enthusiastic, became torrential at times, continued all night.

On the following afternoon Gregorio, taking advantage of the last light before sunset, sat in his bucket chair in front of his home. Gregorio enjoyed a cigarette and read *Siempre*. When he heard hoof beats, slow but steady, he looked up to see two men entering from the north with four burros. Three of the burros carried rocks in sacks on their backs. The other held a man lying limp like a horseshoe over the animal's back.

When they drew close Gregorio realized that two of the burros were his and that the two men on foot were the sons of Ultiminio Huerta.

And as he stared at the procession he saw that the dead man was Ultiminio.

One of the sons glanced at Gregorio but quickly looked away, and the procession continued. Gregorio watched, assumed the men and burros headed for Ultiminio's home, where the sons would deliver their father's body and explain to their mother.

Gregorio entered his home, lighted an oil lamp, and sat

at his table to continue reading. After a respectful wait he would commiserate with Ultiminio's wife and inquire about the cause of her husband's death. He also wanted to know the whereabouts of his other two burros.

"The river had swollen a lot because of the recent rain," Ultiminio's youngest son, Florencio, told Gregorio. "Several times the trail moves from one side of the river to the other, as you know, and we crossed back and forth regularly. Sometimes the water came quite high at the crossings, but we always made it to the other side. When we reached the best place for gathering rocks we stopped and loaded the burros."

Gregorio and Florencio sat on a wooden bench under an almond tree in the plaza.

"Your burros seemed to know when to head downhill, Don Gregorio. So we started back in single file, pleased with our first load, my father near the front. My brother and I walked behind. Two of your burros were natural leaders. Age, I suppose. They obviously were older than the others, but they carried their burdens well."

"Did you load them as heavily as the others?"

"Of course. My father told us to make certain every burro did its part. About a third of the way back your lead burros stumbled a couple of times, but the trail seemed extra-rugged in places. We didn't have any trouble until . . . Where we had to cross the river again . . . It was awful. Water deeper than earlier. Such a rain we'd had." Florencio looked down, inhaled deeply, exhaled, again faced Gregorio.

"Those first two burros couldn't keep their footing in the torrent. Neither could my father." Tears rolled down Florencio's cheeks. He continued through occasional sobs. "The river carried my father downstream. He couldn't swim well. And such a mighty current."

Florencio wiped his face with his handkerchief. "We

found him at the next bend in the river, where fallen tree branches and other debris collected. We could do nothing for him."

"Please except my condolences." Gregorio hesitated. But he had to know. "My burros?"

"Nearby, up against an embankment, drowned. We couldn't even remove the rocks from them. But we dumped the rocks off another burro so we could bring my father home. Such an insult to carry him that way."

"You had no choice." Gregorio, distressed, angry, fought to control his emotions. *I can't hate Ultiminio for betraying my trust, for he's untouchable now. And his sons are not to blame.*

Florencio sniffled, looked at his feet, looked up. "We'll pay you for your loss."

"Florencio, I don't sell dead burros to my friends."

Six months later Don Eustaquio Aguilar, who owned a hale appetite, walked unassisted around the plaza every day, had never been seriously ill, and who at ninety-seven enjoyed a smoke each morning and a sip of whiskey at bedtime, did not awaken from his night's sleep.

Gregorio sat at the table in his small adobe home. His tan sombrero, embroidered in red and with silver conchos around the crown, lay across from him. Twice, neighborhood boys had cleaned and polished his boots, which sat in the corner. Women of the village had washed and ironed his best shirt and pants and mended his coat in case the weather dictated that he wear it. Pencil and paper lay neglected near his hand while he gazed out the front window and tried to organize his thoughts. But women seemed to create a continuous train as they entered through his open front door, greeted him, and joined others in the kitchen, where conversation prospered.

My house is too small for all this commotion. How can they think of so much to talk about? Gregorio picked up his pencil, laid it down, gazed out his front window. *How can I think? What should I write? How can I get anything done?* He walked outside, stood in the middle of the street, inhaled deeply, exhaled. He looked at the little church across the street, surveyed the corn crop on the slope, studied the clouds.

After a few minutes he nodded and returned inside. He sat at his table and picked up his pencil. And Gregorio Santana began writing the speech he must give at the Independence Day celebration the following week. All the attention he'd been receiving annoyed him, also made him nervous. But he knew he had to become accustomed to it, and he felt honored by this business of reigning as patriarch of the mountain village of San Luis.

CANDELARIA

◇◇◇◇◇◇◇◇◇◇◇◇◇◇◇◇◇◇◇◇

Candelaria finished bathing, dried herself, put on her robe, and sat at her dresser. She turned the framed photograph so she could see it better beside her combs and brushes, and she studied it a moment. Candelaria sighed, looked at her face in the mirror, unbraided her hair, and shook it out, long and fine and almost white, so different from forty years ago, and more, when it had been black and shimmering. She began brushing.

And as she brushed she frequently glanced at the photograph, sometimes spoke to the handsome young man standing there so proud and confident.

He had been twenty-three years old, Candelaria nineteen, and they were engaged to marry. A few weeks later when the bull killed him, that photo became her most valuable possession, remained so to this day sixty years later. It evoked loving memories of their mutual hopes and grand times, and it conjured tragic images that tormented her but which she could not avoid nor easily dispel.

On the afternoon he would die, that third Sunday in December of 1905, Pepe Delgado, dressed in a white suit of lights with golden sequins and embroidered gold trim, had ordered the barouche driver to stop by Candelaria's home on their way to the bullring. The driver, a long-ago aspiring bullfighter nicknamed Apizaco who changed ambitions the first time a bull knocked him down, explained later to Candelaria his role in that change of plans.

"'But, Maestro,' I told him, 'it's out of the way. Is there time? Do we dare? We'll be late. You know how bad the Mexico City traffic is on Sunday.' But Pepe smiled and laughed and waved me on. He said, 'Of course we have time. Of course we dare. Have you forgotten that I'm in love?'

"The horses began to fidget and balk when we turned toward your home, Miss Candelaria. They knew we headed the wrong way. Pepe's whole cuadrilla seemed uncomfortable about the detour. But no one said anything."

The maid admitted Pepe. Candelaria's sisters put aside their sewing to laugh and joke with the renowned matador while waiting for Candelaria. When she entered the parlor they stepped into the library but didn't close the door, stood near it to listen.

"You have time to get there," Pepe said. "I fight second and fifth."

"You think I don't know that? The newspapers have touted the corrida all week."

"And that's why I want you to see this corrida. The bulls are beautiful and mine have excellent test notes."

"I've seen beautiful bulls with excellent test notes. They still have horns."

"Yes. You used to go all the time, your whole family. But bulls can't touch me. You know that."

"You're a bullfighter, Pepe. I told you when we became engaged I would never watch you fight again."

"But I had Apizaco bring me out of the way. My whole cuadrilla is waiting."

"I am pleased and flattered. But I'll remain here, praying for you in our chapel, the same as always."

"You might miss the grandest bullfight of the last hundred years."

"I'll take that chance."

"I thought you loved me."

"I do." Candelaria tiptoed and kissed him. "Good luck, Matador."

Pepe hugged her. "I must go. Please be there."

"I'll be with you in my heart."

Pepe nodded, smiled, walked through the entry and down the mansion steps. When he passed the Neptune fountain he halted at the bed of blooming red carnations. Pepe stooped and broke off a long stem. He turned to show Candelaria, watching from the steps. Pepe kissed the carnation and held it to his heart. He inserted the stem inside his frilly white shirt, walked through the gate in the wrought-iron fence surrounding the two-story structure of stone, and climbed into the carriage.

Candelaria watched him while the men of his cuadrilla waved to her, and Apizaco started the horses moving. When the carriage rolled out of sight she returned inside. At 4:00 p.m. she entered the family chapel, where she knelt at a pew and, as always on a day Pepe fought bulls, began addressing the Virgin of Guadalupe.

Pepe's main picador, Zacatecas, brought the word of Pepe's fatal goring. Candelaria sat with her sisters on the living room sofa by the fireplace, though Zacatecas, mentioning his soiled attire, refused a chair. Candelaria promised herself she wouldn't weep until she could be alone.

"As you can see I came straight from the plaza. It happened so quick, Miss. Pepe had been magnificent with his first bull. But with his second, Miss, no less than glorious. All the spectators stood and cheered every pass. I tell you the stands shook with their enthusiasm. Never had Pepe been so artistic and daring and dominating. You should have—just wonderful, Miss.

"The bull had been brave and strong and killed two horses out from under me. As for Pepe, no one had ever seen some of the things he did today. And then for no reason, just a caprice, the bull turned into Pepe and caught him. But, Miss, you probably don't want to hear any more."

"No, Zacatecas, I don't. Thank you so much for coming to me. I know he was your good friend."

"All of us are devastated and in shock, Miss. Pepe had never looked so grand. And no bull had ever touched him before."

Candelaria López, who grew up watching bullfights and loved the colorful but often brutal fiesta, swore to never attend another. Later when developers razed the plaza where Pepe Delgado died she felt mild relief and justice in its destruction. Besides, the Revolution then raging throughout the land dominated her thoughts and everyone else's.

Shortly after insurrectionists occupied the family hacienda in Guanajuato, Gen. Victoriano Huerta confiscated the López mansion for his personal dwelling, and the family moved to a modern two-story house near bustling Avenida Insurgentes Sur. Candelaria placed her photo of Pepe Delgado into a bedroom drawer and married a federal army officer who hated Huerta.

The Revolution touched her more personally again one day when she had just purchased cosmetics at Sanborn's— and several of Zapata's ragged Indians entered and sat nearby at the lunch counter. She trembled and hurried into the street.

When Candelaria's husband fell to a Villista cavalryman's bullet during the fighting at Celaya she returned Pepe's photo to her dresser top.

One sister married a physician and moved to Mazatlán. The other entered a convent. Candelaria lost her parents to the influenza pandemic in 1918 and her second husband, a wealthy merchant, to pneumonia in 1944.

And Candelaria regained her affection for bullfights.

She broke her nonattendance vow in 1945 shortly after a large new bullring opened near Avenida Insurgentes Sur, a short trolley ride and brief walk for her. Sundays had become so boring except for church. A bullfight would chase away the ennui.

Almost from the start of her renewed enthusiasm for the fiesta of the bulls Candelaria preferred a small outside table at Restaurante El Ruedo. It sat on narrow Avenida Máximo Camacho fronting the bullring and drew large crowds of excited customers before and after each corrida.

Candelaria arrived early to claim the same spot before someone took it, but waiters soon remembered her and began saving her a table. She sipped a glass of Manzanilla, loved the brassy music from the mariachis inside the restaurant, and watched the fans entering the bullring. On the table in front of her each Sunday lay the daily *El Esto* with its bullfight news and beside it a bunch of fresh red carnations bound by green ribbon with a large bow. She always purchased the flowers to pitch to a matador enjoying a triumphant afternoon. During inclement weather she sat inside El Ruedo at a window and hoped the skies would clear. Or she stayed home.

After many years of her routine Candelaria recognized most of the regular fans, many of whom paused at her table to greet her, often by name. They saw an elderly woman, handsome, aristocratic, in a black dress and with a white silk mantilla covering much of her long silvery hair. She had become a welcome fixture, part of a bullfight Sunday.

"Who gets your carnations today, Candelaria?" someone usually asked.

"We'll have to wait and see, won't we?"

"The young fellow making his debut might be the one today."

"The papers write about him a lot," she said. "But this is not the provinces."

Before long when an older fan greeted her Candelaria began asking if he knew about Pepe Delgado, perhaps even saw Pepe fight bulls.

"Sorry. Never heard of him," became a common reply.

"Must be from before my time," she heard frequently.

"Didn't he get killed in Spain a few years ago?"

"Oh, no," she said. "Not Pepe."

The most satisfying reply, though infrequent, would be when an old-timer said something like, "I've read a little about him. Did you know him?"

Disappointed, Candelaria answered only, "For a little while."

One Sunday a few weeks before Candelaria's eightieth birthday an older waiter new to her approached. He addressed her as "Missus" and said to call him Hermenegildo. She ordered her usual glass of pale dry sherry. He thanked her and left.

When Hermenegildo returned he set her wine down, examined her carnations, smiled, and lingered. "There'll be plenty of competition for your flowers today, Missus." He glanced at the poster in the nearby window.

Candelaria also looked at it: "7th big corrida of the 1965–1966 season" and the names of the matadors and bull ranch. She again faced the waiter. "You're new. But you know about me and the carnations."

"Everyone knows about the beautiful Candelaria and the splendid bouquet of red carnations she awards."

"Well, the carnations are beautiful. And the young men

are splendid." She paused, examined the waiter, tall and slim and near her age. "You must have been working somewhere else."

"Down the street. But always around the bullring."

"Tell me." Candelaria inhaled deeply, exhaled. She had been so disappointed over the years, hesitated to ask, but continued. "By any chance is it possible you've heard of Pepe Delgado?"

"Of course. Who hasn't, in my age group?"

"Seems like many haven't, Hermenegildo. Please go on. Tell me."

"There's so much, Missus. In all the cantinas and cafes, the parks, even in church, or at least before and after services, everyone talked about Pepe, so good, so graceful, dominating. We used to joke that his bulls were trained. And, oh, the risks that young man took. Missus, Pepe Delgado was the greatest matador of his time. Everyone said the bulls couldn't touch him. Everyone called him the man they could not kill." He paused.

"Were you there the day he died?"

"Yes, just a young fellow, ran errands, did odd jobs. I didn't have much money so I always sat in the cheap seats, high in the sun, saw him fight many times. I can still envision the bull catching him that day in 1905. It happened so fast. None of us could believe it." Hermenegildo shook his head. "Did you know him? Were you there too?"

"I knew him well. No, I stayed home to pray for him. My fiancé."

He touched her shoulder. "I'm sorry. Would you like more wine?"

"Oh, no. Hermenegildo, I have such a wonderful feeling to hear that you know about Pepe and saw him fight. It's how I felt years ago when I could still talk to men and women who had known my parents. Will you always wait on me here?"

"Count on it." He motioned toward the bullring. "His statue should be up there on top of the wall with the others."

"I guess whoever built the thing never heard of Pepe."

"He's been gone so long."

"On Sundays," Candelaria said, "it doesn't seem so long ago, and especially not this Sunday." She glanced across the street at the crowd in front of the ticket windows. "Because you know all about Pepe."

When Candelaria stood and picked up her flowers Hermenegildo arrived at her side. "I look forward to waiting on you afterwards."

While taking her regular seat in the front row on the shady side of the arena Candelaria exchanged greetings with numerous other spectators. After the participants marched across the sand a matador approached along the alley, a passage slightly lower than the front-row seats. He stopped in front of Candelaria, looked up, and tossed his parade cape onto the railing in front of her. Adjacent fans helped spread it on the fence.

"Thank you, Manuel." She leaned forward to speak with him more easily. "I hope your bulls are good."

"One has excellent notes, the other so-so. We'll see."

"How good is this fellow calling himself The Earthquake?"

"I don't know about an earthquake, but he should do all right."

When he stepped away, Candelaria recalled the time a few years earlier when from that same seat she had caught the attention of this bullfighter, Manuel Capetillo, as he walked by. She had done the same thing with other matadors, her question always identical, the answer virtually unchanged.

"Excuse me. But have you heard of Pepe Delgado?"

"No, Missus. Is he a bullfighter?"

And she would smile feebly and sit back in disappointment.

But Capetillo had given Candelaria the answer she craved. "So long ago, Missus. But, sure, born in Jalisco, same as me, Guadalajara, I believe. My grandfather saw him fight before Pepe moved to Mexico City, told me all about him."

She felt tears of joy on her cheeks.

During Capetillo's long career she often chatted with him, won his friendship and cherished it. When he learned of her lost love he consoled her. "Don't be discouraged because today's bullfighters haven't heard of Pepe," he told her. "They discuss today's bulls but don't read anything except bullfight publications and the movie listings."

On this afternoon, as custom dictated, Capetillo ceded his first bull to the newcomer, thereby welcoming young Juan Retana into bullfighting's hierarchy. And The Earthquake performed so marvelously that when he circled the arena the band played *Silverio* and two other fast-moving tunes.

When Juan Retana arrived near Candelaria she tossed him her bouquet of red carnations. One of his aides caught it and handed it to him.

"He didn't acknowledge you," the man next to Candelaria said.

"He's too excited. But I'm happy for him."

Capetillo found his first bull so difficult to handle that Candelaria had just decided he should end the act without trying to do well when the bull bumped him, knocked him down, and rolled him around.

She caught her breath, sobbed silently: Pepe Delgado lay bleeding on that sand.

Women screamed and men yelled before others in the arena distracted the animal. Capetillo stood, battered but unbloodied.

Candelaria wiped her eyes, no longer saw a bull attacking Pepe.

Later in the afternoon when Capetillo's second bull galloped into the arena Candelaria judged it to be the better of his two. When he stepped onto the sand to greet it she saw Capetillo's fire, his art, and determination. Bull and man performed magnificently. Capetillo won both ears and the tail.

The band played *Guadalajara* and *Jalisco, No Te Rajes*.

Alfredo Leal, tall and handsome, fared well with his two bulls.

Capetillo soon walked along the passageway and stopped in front of Candelaria while an aide took down his parade cape.

"I'm sorry I gave away my carnations too soon, Manuel."

"It's all right. I should have done even better, that bull had been so outstanding. You should see me in Guadalajara."

When she climbed toward the exit Candelaria noticed a young woman carrying a bouquet of red carnations bound by a green ribbon. *Maybe someday he'll recognize me if he lasts long enough.* Candelaria sighed, exchanged comments with others exiting, and stepped into the tunnel leading to the street.

Surrounded by the mash of fans leaving the bullring, a black Mercedes sedan also trying to reach daylight crawled along that same tunnel. But when the car drew alongside Candelaria it stopped, and Manuel Capetillo called to her through a backseat window. "Candelaria, I want you to meet my new picador." Capetillo motioned to the young man beside him.

She looked, saw the picador's tan canvaslike pants, embroidered heavy black jacket, his hat like an upside-down wash basin in his lap.

Capetillo introduced him by name and added, "We call him Zacatecas."

The young man ran his fingers through wavy black hair damp with perspiration.

Candelaria gasped.

"His family is a dynasty of picadors nicknamed Zacatecas." Capetillo smiled at him. "This young fellow is Zacatecas the Fourth or Fifth, no?"

"The Fifth. So pleased to meet you, Mrs. Candelaria. All my life I've heard about you and that awful day and how my ancestor brought you the terrible news."

Candelaria nodded, wiped her eyes. She wished she could hug the young man, that direct link to Pepe Delgado.

"All my people knew Pepe Delgado in those days," Zacatecas V said. "They called him the man they could not kill." He paused. "Excuse me, Missus. I should not have said that. Not true anyway."

Candelaria nodded. "Young man, I'm not so sure about that. Not sure at all."

The Mercedes rolled ahead.

Stunned—by pleasure? gratitude? loneliness?—Candelaria stepped to the wall, leaned against it, wiped her eyes while the crowd passed. In a moment, familiar nostalgia enveloped her. She felt her spirit returning.

Candelaria headed for El Ruedo. She would sip one more Manzanilla and rest before walking to the trolley stop.

Then she would head home and look forward to when it would be Sunday one more time.

A Black Suit for Cipriano

They lingered at the cemetery. Even though they had gone there often in the year since a neighbor's mule kicked him in the head and killed him, they stalled, for now they would abandon their village to face uncertainties in the city. A return trip could not be arranged frequently.

"Maybe we can come back next year for the Day of the Dead," Magdalena had told her sons and daughter. She wiped her eyes.

Her husband's parents and grandparents, his brothers and sisters, also rested in that cemetery of their mountain hamlet, Mil Piedras. He had found Magdalena in a distant village and brought her there, and now she had told the children they would be better off in the city.

"Take a last look, children." She motioned to the flowers on his grave. "Then let's go home and pack."

They sat at the kitchen table. Cardboard boxes stacked in a corner of their three-room rustic shack held their clothes, a baseball glove, Carmela's doll, Magdalena's wedding photo, an outdated calendar portraying the Virgin of Guadalupe, and another, also outdated, carrying a likeness of Cuauhté-moc. Rope bound the boxes for easy carrying.

"I don't want to go," sixteen-year-old Cipriano said.

"I agree," Garcilaso, two years younger, said.

"We all go," Magdalena told him. "We need to stay together."

"Let's stay together here." Cipriano stood, walked to the door, and looked out.

"Yes," Carmela said. "All my friends are here."

"Mine too." Garcilaso nodded at their mother.

"Children, we've been through all this."

They waited for the moment to tote their belongings to the central square of Mil Piedras and occupy benches on the open-sided jungle bus, which would carry them to the highway at Tepic. There they could take the modern bus to Guadalajara.

Cipriano sipped coffee from his paper cup, wished their treasured ceramic mugs had not been packed, examined the interior of their small home, its walls of tree branches and palm-frond spines, the roof of tin covered by palm fronds. He examined their sleeping mats rolled up beside the boxes. "We'll need a better home than this in Guadalajara. It gets cold there."

"Not so much," Magdalena said. "Just at night some." She could handle the Spanish almost as well as her children, occasionally read well-perused copies of *Alarma* and *Impacto*, magazines the jungle bus driver, a friend of her late husband, passed on to them.

"I can't go without a black suit," Cipriano said.

"Why do you need a black suit?"

"To get a good job. I can't make a living in the city picking coconuts."

"But you can't get a black suit, any suit, unless we start over in Guadalajara." Cipriano studied his mother, mostly Indian, beautiful in her mid-thirties, knew she had more reasons to leave Mil Piedras than the death of his father. His friends had told him, and he had learned from his own observations. *The women here resent her, maybe even hate her, because she's prettier than they are, because their husbands and boyfriends smile at her too much when they pass, and because she's an outsider from that far-off village where my father discovered her while working in the area.*

"The peddler is due through here in a few weeks," Cipriano said. "Let's wait."

"He offers cloth and thread and kitchen utensils. I need a sewing machine to make a suit."

Cipriano finished his coffee. "If I had a suit I could land a job and buy you one."

"You're a good worker." Magdalena patted his hand. "You'll thrive in the city. But we have to start with what we have. It's the same for everyone who goes there from a village."

Cipriano knew what people, not just his mother, said about him: works hard, enterprising, strong and fast and handsome. One friend's mother said that if Cipriano were a highwayman the women he robbed would give up more than their jewels, do so with a smile. He sighed. "I wonder what kind of work I'll find."

"We'll see. We'll be like pioneers, explorers."

"What about me?" Garcilaso said.

"You'll enroll in secondary school. But you can find something part time. Carmela will be in first grade. She can help me after class. We'll sew and wash and cook for neighbors."

Carmela extended her arms on the table and made fists. She frowned. "My friends . . ."

"You'll get wrinkles making such a face." Magdalena stood. "I think I hear the bus."

They left the modern bus at the first barrio it entered, a congregation of incondite homes of scrap lumber and corrugated tin and tar paper, a few of adobe. A sign at the side of the highway said downtown Guadalajara waited three kilometers ahead. Others on nearby buildings advertised beer and soft drinks, while the symbol of a major political party dominated a short adobe wall deteriorating at both ends.

"That looks like a little store." Cipriano pointed to the shack supporting the beer advertisement. "Let's see what they say."

Their investigation sent them two blocks along a dirt street that widened around a water faucet opposite the adobe home of the local political chief, the cacique, Juan Robles.

Where are you from? That's mostly Indians, isn't it? Where are you going? Why did you stop at Salsipuedes? Where is your husband?

The questions angered Cipriano. So did the way the cacique looked at his mother.

But Magdalena smiled and answered, and Juan Robles told them of a vacant home three dwellings east of the water faucet.

"You're lucky," he said. "They just moved to the city, said I could do what I wanted with the furniture."

"Perhaps we could use it." Magdalena looked in the shack's direction.

"It's three large rooms with a wood-burning stove. An outdoor toilet is in the back. Let me see." He examined some papers on his desk, nodded, and smiled. "For the furniture and stove, and the right to occupy, it's yours for only a hundred pesos."

"We're awfully low on funds," Magdalena said.

"It's a one-time payment, not monthly. We're all squatters here."

"I think we should look around."

"Everything in Salsipuedes has to clear through me. It's the only one available that's suitable for you. It's close to the water and the highway."

"I don't know."

Juan Robles hesitated and smiled. "All right. For you seventy-five pesos."

"Fifty."

"Sixty-five."

Again, Cipriano disliked the way the cacique looked at his mother.

But Magdalena paid, and they carried their belongings toward their new home.

"We're going to have trouble with that fatso."

"I can handle him, Cipri."

"You saw how he looked at you."

"How could I miss it? I almost laughed out loud."

"What are you talking about, Mama?"

"Just life, Garci."

Cipriano said, "I'll order him to stay away from you."

"I can handle him." Magdalena took his arm with her free hand.

"I didn't like him either," Carmela said.

"We're going to give this place a try," Magdalena told her children.

"What a name," Cipriano said. "'Salsipuedes.' Why couldn't we find a barrio named for Pancho Villa or Zapata?"

They considered the stove a luxury, for few homes had one. The dwellings with electricity stood on the far edges to the north, where enterprising residents spliced into municipal power lines.

"These tiny rooms certainly aren't 'large,'" Magdalena said.

She purchased material from a neighbor and made Carmela a black skirt and white blouse like the other girls wore to school. And her skills with needle and thread plus the variety of foods she created at her stove soon attracted clients from throughout the barrio.

Cipriano hitchhiked or walked into the city each day in search of work and never failed to remind his mother he needed a black suit in order to acquire a decent job.

Garcilaso walked Carmela to the primary school each day, continued to his own classes in the secondary, and met her after class to escort her home. Along the way, for their mother's stove they collected wood and tree branches from beside the highway.

On a day when he roamed farther than usual Garcilaso discovered the edge of the pine forest, where he found plenty of firewood. When Cipriano helped him one weekend they gathered enough to sell to other residents of Salsipuedes. They gave their earnings to their mother, who deposited the money into a three-pound coffee can in the kitchen. But Cipriano continued to dedicate his weekdays to his hunt for employment in the city.

"When the can is full," Cipriano asked, "may I buy a black suit with some of the money?"

"It will never be full," Magdalena said, "because it's needed for groceries."

"But someday it might," Garcilaso said, "and Cipri needs money for his suit."

"Carmelita needs a backpack to carry her books," Magdalena said.

"Couldn't you make her one? For me too?"

"Not without a sewing machine, Garci. Because of the heavy material required, my stitching would embarrass you both."

"I'll look for a good used sewing machine in the city," Cipriano said."

"When we can afford it, Cipri. Meanwhile watch for the old type with a treadle for my foot. We don't have electricity."

Carmela said, "Why didn't we get a house with electricity? Our teacher in Mil Piedras said TV has cartoons in color every Saturday morning."

"This had been the only place available. Besides we can't afford a TV."

"But when we can . . ." Carmela looked at Cipriano.

"And I heard there's a cowboy show called *The Lone Ranger*," Garcilaso said.

"I'll look for a TV too," Cipriano told them.

They had finished breakfast on Saturday two weeks later and sat sipping coffee at the table when Cipriano heard tapping on the front door. He went to open it, stood immobile, stunned by her smile, her beauty.

"Cipri, what's got into you?" Magdalena rose and reached the doorway just as Cipriano finally stepped aside. She introduced the visitor to her sons. Consuelo María Espinosa already knew Carmelita. "Sit with us, Concha."

Cipriano offered his chair, took his coffee, and leaned against the kitchen counter. He had heard his mother talk of this neighbor, a young woman her age, not as dark, sophisticated, ambitious, who with laughter had told Magdalena of the cacique's awkward advances.

"I pat him on his bald head and walk away," Concha had said.

And Cipriano leaned against the counter and studied her: tight black pants, boots to mid-calf, pleated white blouse, red bolero jacket, long silken black hair, lips like a juicy red apple, wise eyes aged beyond her years.

"Concha is going to show me around the city someday," Magdalena said. "She knows Guadalajara like I know my frying pan."

Concha laughed, waving away the praise.

Cipriano nodded. *Yes, I bet she does.*

Garcilaso and Carmela excused themselves and entered a bedroom.

"Do your homework," Magdalena said. She poured coffee for Concha, and Cipriano moved to the table. But an occasional mumble became his only participation despite Concha and his mother frequently glancing at him while they talked, as though inviting him to comment. And he sipped his coffee and studied Concha while the women chatted.

"Maybe next Saturday you can go into town with me," Concha said.

"We'll see," Magdalena said. "We're still getting established."

"But you haven't been even once?"

"Cipriano goes. He's looking for work, and he tells me about the beautiful buildings, the monument to the famous men, the parks, the fountains."

"Not the nightclubs, I bet." Concha smiled at Cipriano. "There are a lot of good shows. Paloma San Basilio is at one club, José Ramón Jiménez at another." She turned back to Magdalena. "And of course the museums and art galleries and the beautiful Basílica de Guadalajara. I'll probably stay over tonight and catch a Mass tomorrow before returning. Anything to get out of this barrio for a while. I'm saving to escape permanently."

"Do you do that often? I mean, stay over?"

"Oh sure. A nice hotel. A hot bath. A good bed."

"Isn't that expensive?"

"Remember? My husband left me some money. And I have . . . friends."

Cipriano caught her hesitation, her wink at his mother.

Concha soon excused herself. "Thanks for the visit. May I bring you some mending on my way to catch the bus?"

"Of course. And I'll try to go with you as soon as I make myself a new dress."

"You're beautiful. You'll fit right in." Concha smiled at Cipriano. "Your son is quite handsome. Better keep him at home. Some city girl might capture him."

Cipriano stood, watched Concha leave.

"Isn't she nice, Cipri?"

"Mama, I don't want you involved with her."

"What do you mean? We chat. Is that 'involved'?"

"Her world is different from ours, from yours." He sat.

"I've never been to a nightclub. I might not even like it."

"What if you do?"

"I suppose I go once in a while."

"Mama, I've seen her type. She'll get you in trouble."

Magdalena smiled. "So you're an expert on women?" She touched Cipriano's hand. "Concha's become a good friend already. We have long talks about everything, and she's helping me improve my Spanish. I never had such a friend when we lived in Mil Piedras."

"That's nice, Mama. But have her friendship here, not in Guadalajara at night."

"You worry too much. I'll be all right. Concha will be with me."

Cipriano discovered several job possibilities for a strong young man who didn't object to physical labor, such as delivering bottled water throughout the barrios or working in construction. But he knew that even if he rose to the top in one of those toils he wouldn't be happy. He wanted a job in a business, where he could have a career. When he heard that waiters received little pay, though they earned tips, he decided that would be good work for a start.

But he had trouble obtaining it.

"Every place I apply," he told his mother, "they turn me down. Either they don't have an opening or they say I lack experience."

"Did you try nice restaurants? Expensive-looking ones?"

"Sure. Some. The pay and tips would be better. Nobody has wanted me."

"Find a modest place away from the glamour. Obtain some experience and try again." Magdalena reached into the can on the kitchen counter and withdrew several coins. "Get yourself a factory-made shirt that doesn't need ironing. People will see the difference. And a haircut."

"Can we afford it?"

"We have to."

"We're saving to get a bicycle so Garci can make deliveries."

"He can wait a little."

The first time Cipriano wore his new shirt he found work at the humble Restaurante La Esperanza three blocks from the Teatro Degollado. He started at 6:00 a.m. and worked until 10:00 p.m. with a three-hour midafternoon siesta break. Offerings featured tacos of goat or beef, cheese enchiladas, pozole, and menudo. Clientele included salesgirls from popular clothing shops and the five-and-dime around the corner, laborers from various projects in the vicinity, and young Americans male and female ordering in English or chopped-up Spanish. Cipriano received little pay and seldom saw a generous tip, but he enjoyed free meals.

Every other day while Magdalena washed his new shirt he wore a homemade one, but the boss liked him and didn't object.

One day during a lull Cipriano approached him. "How long will I have to work here to afford a new black suit?"

The owner, chopping onions on the grill, looked up and nodded. "You don't need a suit to work here."

"No. Just in general."

"You mean girls. Maybe six months if you get good tips."

"I haven't seen a good one yet."

The owner laughed and returned to his onions.

During his long break Cipriano wandered the streets, went to the Biblioteca Benjamín Franklin to read magazines, and found a vacant lot a fifteen-minute walk away where boys his age played soccer. They welcomed him, and he joined them several times because his skills matched theirs. Then he didn't play anymore for fear he would dirty or tear his clothes.

Returning home one night after his third week at La Esperanza he could tell by wavering brightness in the front window that his mother had lighted candles. Cipriano reached the door just as the cacique opened it. Cipriano tensed, became angry.

Juan Robles faced into the room. "As you wish, Missus." He turned and bumped into Cipriano, excused himself, and kept walking.

"I told you we would have trouble with him, Mama."

"And I told you I could handle him. And I just did."

"Why did you let him in?"

"I expected it to be you. When I saw otherwise I felt I had to invite him in to see what he wanted. He's the boss around here, remember."

"What did he want?"

"Some excuse about bottled-water delivery starting here."

"It should taste better than from the faucet in the street. Did he harm you?"

"Of course not, Cipri. He's not mean, just clumsy."

"I don't like it."

"He won't bother me again. How did work go?"

"The usual. I've been there long enough. I need a black suit so I can dress up to apply at better places."

"Maybe not. Get another store-bought shirt so you'll have a clean one every day."

"What about Garci's bicycle?"

"We have enough now for that too."

"Mama, even if I get a good job as waiter there has to be something better I can do, some office work or maybe sales, something where I can get ahead."

Magdalena put her arm around him. "Time for bed. Remember when you were happy climbing trees barefoot to pick coconuts?"

"How could I forget?"

When he stopped by the soccer field he told the boys he merely wanted to say hello and watch. "I need to spend my break hunting for a better job."

"What kind of work you looking for?" This came from a tall boy nicknamed the Signer because he left a signature symbol with the graffiti he painted on walls public and private.

"Waiter in a top restaurant. They say tips are great."

"And the work hard." The Signer nodded at the other youths nearby. "You could make some money with us tonight. There's a truck that delivers meat to butcher shops. We highjack it, sell the meat at a discount to places we know, take some good cuts home."

"I don't think so, Signer." Cipriano looked at two boys kicking a ball in the background, the larger a mugger known as Knuckles, the other a shoplifter called Fingers.

A youth nicknamed Swifty said, "We know how fast you can run. Come with me tonight." He picked pockets for a living, could run almost as fast as Cipriano.

"I'd better check out some more restaurants." Cipriano smiled and moved away.

But he didn't find work at any of them, soon had to resume toil at La Esperanza.

Late one night when Cipriano stepped off the bus at

Salsipuedes he recognized a well-dressed woman leaving a taxi across the highway under the street light at the barrio entry, Consuelo María Espinosa. Another woman also left the taxi, Cipriano's mother. He remained in darkness beside the highway until Concha and Magdalena disappeared among the one-story huts.

Only at breakfast and on Sundays like this could the family be together, reporting on their activities, unfolding plans for the day. They sat now at the table consuming scrambled eggs sprinkled with goat cheese, with pork chorizo and corn tortillas on the side, Carmela and Garcilaso drinking milk, Magdalena and Cipriano coffee.

Carmela for the third time thanked Cipriano for the backpack he'd given her, and he again apologized because it had been used.

"But it looks new, Cipri," Carmela said. "No one can tell. How did you find it?"

"A friend named Fingers got it for me cheap. I met him playing soccer on my break." Cipriano looked away, thinking about his mother arriving late at night in a taxi with Concha.

Garcilaso praised his brother for cleaning, oiling, and painting his bicycle and for affixing a large crate behind the seat so Garcilaso could carry more than he could hold with one arm. He wore his new-looking backpack. "I'm getting a lot of customers for wood and groceries. Everyone admires my bike."

"Be careful on the highway." Cipriano sipped his coffee.

When his siblings left the table to work a picture puzzle he continued sitting, looking out the window, turning his coffee mug in a circle.

Magdalena refilled his mug and hers and sat. "What is it, Cipri?"

"Nothing."

"What else?" She smiled. "You're so grim and silent, like something died in you."

He disliked confronting his mother about what obviously had been a visit to Guadalajara with Concha, felt he should, but feared what he might learn. *Let it go for another time.* "Nothing, Mama." He sipped his coffee, raised his eyes to see her look cemented on him.

"Want any more breakfast, Cipri?"

He shook his head.

"I'm going to." She stood, placed chorizo on a tortilla, rolled the tortilla, and resat.

Cipriano watched her take a bite. He looked out the window. *I can't do this. But I must.*

His stomach knotted, palms perspired. *Jesús, María, and José.*

Magdalena took another bite, chewed, and swallowed. "Cipri, don't you notice anything different about me?"

I do but I can't describe it. I told you not to go to town with that woman. "I don't know. It's something."

"It's my hair." Magdalena touched her coiffure. "You men are all alike. Look, Cipri." Now she had both hands on her coiffure.

"Oh. I hadn't noticed. It's nice."

"My first professional hairdo." She started talking fast, animated. "Concha convinced me to go to town with her. She says the beauty shop she goes to is as good as the fancy ones and a lot cheaper. A cousin owns it. Then we went shopping. Well, window shopping. Except one store near the Plaza Mayor. All the best shops are on or near the plaza or on Avenida Juárez. That's what Concha says. We walked under so many beautiful arcades. Concha says they're Colonial, the basílica too. I got to select a dress. I made a small down payment, and when I get it paid off I can have it. They call it 'layaway.' I can give you the money and maybe you'll stop by and make the payments?"

"Sure, Mama." *But that didn't take half the night.*

"I've never had a store-bought dress. I'll wear it to Mass. We grabbed a snack and I thought we'd start home. But Concha told me about a club where they have an early show, and she said the doorman would give us good seats because he was her cousin. I didn't think my dress looked nice enough, but Concha said I looked fine, that the place wasn't fancy. We sipped orange pop and watched for a long time. Just wonderful, the singers, the dancers. I'd never seen a live show except for when the masked wrestlers came to Mil Piedras that time. You were little but you saw them too."

"I remember, Mama." He slid back in his chair, extended his feet.

"Concha seemed to know the waiters so we didn't have to pay anything. But you have to stay up so late, especially for the big stars. I don't want to go again. It's not the life for me."

His stomach unknotted. His palms stopped sweating. "I'm happy for you, Mama."

"I knew you wouldn't mind." Magdalena stepped into her bedroom and returned with a slip of paper. "Concha says give you this."

"What's it mean, this name and address?"

"It's a restaurant. Not five stars, as they say, but good. It's near the Hotel Fénix, one of the best places. It's much better than where you're working."

"I don't want to be in debt to her."

"It's for all of us, Cipri. Just join the union when they tell you. Big tips. Good clientele. Concha says tell the manager she sent you. Her cousin owns it."

He sighed. "Maybe I'll earn enough to get a black suit quicker."

An ambulance brought Garcilaso's body home in the early evening a few days later. The police told Magdalena the bus driver hadn't been able to see the boy on the bicycle because of the dark.

"We had to ask so many people to learn where to bring him," a policeman said.

By the time Cipriano returned home, neighbors had helped console his mother and sister and had cleaned the blood from the back of Garcilaso's head. Except for the head wound, he couldn't see any damage to his brother's body. When Cipriano cried, his mother and sister hugged him, and they cried together.

Cipriano skipped work the next day and sought out a funeral home Juan Robles directed him to in the western outskirts of the city. "You have to get him in the ground quickly," the cacique said. "How about a funeral Mass? The parish church is just down the road."

Cipriano descended from the bus near the mortuary and from the funeral director obtained prices of coffins and burial plots. The prices stunned him. He rode the next bus into central Guadalajara, walked across the Plaza Mayor to the basílica, and inquired about a funeral Mass for Garcilaso. The cost saddened him. He walked out.

At home in the late afternoon he sat with his mother and sister at the kitchen table and reported on his findings.

"We don't have anywhere near that much money, Cipri."

"I know, Mama."

Carmela started crying.

"In Mil Piedras we just put people in the ground, didn't pay for nothing."

"Life is different in the city, Mama."

"You mean death."

"Death too."

"For the burial," Cipriano said, "we could save money, buy just the five-year plan."

Carmela asked, "Why is it called that?"

"After five years the bodies are dug up and dumped into a corner of the cemetery with others whose family couldn't afford perpetuity."

"What's per-pet—?"

"Forever," Magdalena said.

Carmela sobbed.

Magdalena hugged her. "Don't worry. We'll find a way. How much for the Mass?"

He told her.

"We'd better try the parish church."

"Garci deserves the basílica, Mama."

"Of course. But such a high cost."

"They're booked up anyway for a while. I have time to look around."

"I could take over Garci's deliveries," Carmela said.

"You're too little," Magdalena said. "Besides, we don't have a bicycle anymore."

Cipriano leaned forward. "Can't it be repaired?"

"The police say someone stole it from the scene. I had to pay the ambulance too."

Cipriano caught an early bus the next morning, left it near the mortuary to make a deposit for a coffin and burial plot, again rode the next bus to the Plaza Mayor, and at the Basílica de Guadalajara chatted at length with the arrangements director. Cipriano smelled incense, heard a choir singing. The director reeked of an antiperspirant overdose.

"My brother lived a good Christian life," Cipriano said. "He was only fourteen. He wanted to go to seminary and become the best priest ever."

"I'm sure. But I told you about the costs. The Mass you want is considered deluxe."

"I never heard of such a thing. A Mass is a Mass."

"You're a provincial. You don't know anything about the city."

More than you think, mister. I have friends who could disappear your silver candlesticks overnight, your medicinal wine too. "My brother never did a bad thing in his life."

The director shuffled papers.

"He did all kinds of work to help our mother and sister."

"Admirable."

"He never missed school or Sunday Mass."

The director looked at Cipriano. "I've mentioned our prices."

Cipriano clenched his fists, spun about, and hurried outside. *Oily bastard.* He walked under the portals on the other side of the plaza, crossed the square, fists in his pants pockets, wandered without plan. He felt like a vagabond.

When Cipriano reached a small park filled by royal poincianas bursting with blooms scarlet and orange he sat on a bench in the shade to think. He sat for a long time, considered every adult he'd come to know. *Maybe Concha has a cousin who could help.* He laughed at himself, but distress continued to burden him.

And he thought about Signer and Fingers, about Knuckles and Swifty.

After a while Cipriano stood. He realized what he must do.

"Garci looks so nice, so alive," Magdalena said. "And the flowers, so kind of the neighbors, and them every bit as poor as us."

"Maybe Concha spent some of her savings."

"Don't make fun of her, Cipri. She's my good friend."

"Mine too," Carmela said. "She helps me with my homework."

Magdalena looked around. "People are leaving. Now we go to the cemetery?"

"The mortician said give them a few days, Mama."

"I never heard of that."

"They're waiting for the stonecutter. They say it's the custom here."

"Are you sure you had enough money to pay for permanent burial?"

"Very permanent, Mama."

"I'm hungry," Carmela said. "And this mortuary is creepy." She tugged the sleeve of Cipriano's newly purchased black suit. "Let's go."

Cipriano had bought the suit at a side-street shop Concha recommended. "They'll treat you right," she had said. "The proprietor is my cousin."

Three weeks later when they arrived at the basílica for the funeral Mass the arrangements director hurried to intercept them and offer condolences.

"My son tells me you gave us a big discount on the Mass. Thank you so much."

"Your son drives a hard bargain. He will become a top salesman or diplomat."

They entered the nave and headed for a front pew, where they joined Concha, Juan Robles, and a few other neighbors. "The man seemed so kind." Magdalena sat next to Concha.

Very kind, all right," Cipriano mused, *thanks to a modest bribe and my promise from Signer that the silver candelabra and Madonna from Colonial days would miraculously reappear. Crazy guys. I guess they didn't have time to grab the wine.* His suit fitted well. Cipriano made certain the back of the coat did not get wrinkled against the pew.

"I wish they'd finish the grave marker so we could go to the cemetery."

"Soon, Mama. They say the stonecutter's been awfully busy."

Carmela tugged Concha's arm. "Cipri's black suit makes him look like a movie star."

"He already did." Concha smiled at him.

Cipriano also smiled, happy within, pleased with himself. *The groundskeeper didn't want much money. Once the cenotaph is in place we'll go to the graveyard, and Mama will never know that Garci isn't there. And I'll get a full refund on the coffin, thanks to Knuckles and the Signer visiting the mortician with me.*

He continued smiling, recalling the other help Signer and friends gave him. The director of the new medical school had balked at first. But he didn't want the building's walls covered with graffiti that would include damaging comments. And he seemed to tremble when Signer hinted that pharmaceuticals had a way of disappearing.

So the director paid for Garcilaso's remains, a young, virtually undamaged cadaver, paid generously instead of demanding it be donated, according to custom.

ISABELA

◇◇◇◇◇◇◇◇◇◇◇◇◇

Ever since friends had carried her father home that morning because a tree branch laden with mangoes fell on his head and killed him, sixteen-year-old Isabela knew her fate.

She hated it.

No one mentioned it that afternoon before or during the burial service, which the shaman and one of the village elders conducted. After they sprinkled incense and certain herbs into his rustic, hastily constructed wooden coffin and nailed it shut, four men lowered Agapito Ortega into the ground at the graveyard uphill from the village of San Lucas.

Isabela and her siblings entered the small adobe chapel, briefly prayed to an amateurish oil painting of the Virgin of Guadalupe and to a hand-carved crucifix, and lit candles. Their mother and grandfather waited with the shaman near the open entry. When Isabela turned and glanced their way she caught the shaman scowling at her.

However, at a family gathering that evening in their home of tightly woven palm frond spines roofed by palm fronds laid thickly over sheets of tin she saw the shaman calm and authoritative. And she felt trampled and diminished when he divined in a mystic revelation that it would be best for all of them. And her grandfather ordered it.

"You have to go," Little Grandfather said.

"But I don't want to."

"It won't be forever," he said, "and you can visit us regularly."

Isabela, careful to not sound disrespectful, said, "This isn't fair."

"Your mother or I will escort you down the mountain tomorrow."

And so Isabela must go to one of the houses on the outskirts of the small city at the rim of the great bay to toil with the girls and young women there.

The shaman sealed his participation in Isabela's destiny by presenting Little Grandfather with a shiny jaguar's tooth and the dried-and-pressed wing tip of an eagle. "Send these amulets along with Isabela for protection." He stepped into the night.

"It's only for maybe a year," her mother told Isabela. "Because you're pretty you'll earn so much money we'll be all right until your brothers can do man's work."

"But, Mama, a year is so long."

"The time will go swiftly, a hawk diving on a rabbit."

"Or slow, a snail crossing the trail."

"You'll be all right, Isabelita."

"What if I don't like it?"

"I can tell you right now you won't. But you get accustomed to it."

That night during a light rain they sat at the kitchen table: Isabela; her two sisters and two brothers, all younger than Isabela; their mother; and their mother's father, Little Grandfather.

Isabela could still smell the shaman's incense, recall the mystery in his eyes. *Or was it wisdom? Or power?* "Maybe we should talk to the priest. Papa would like that."

"The priest won't come to our village again for nearly a month," her mother said. "Our situation is urgent. Your father tried to influence us because he never liked the old ways. But you've always preferred the shaman over the priest."

"I know. He doesn't talk on and on. But sometimes his eyes confuse me."

"Isabelita, I'm too old to do much," Little Grandfather said. "Your brothers and sisters can gather firewood and fruit with me to trade for an occasional frying chicken or suckling pig. Maybe we can trap birds. But even with our little garden, that's about all."

"I understand that part, Little Grandfather, but I . . ." Isabela looked through the door, into the night. "All my friends are here. And it's such a long walk. And the men—"

"You'll make new friends," her mother said. "One of us will bring you to visit when we have time. We'll ride one burro and lead the other. We'll find out which day."

"If I have to do this, a Sunday would be best to come home."

"You have to go. You've heard me talk of Maritza Villalobos? Moved to the next village when she was young? She worked in the second-class house for two years. She told me these things before she left. Maritza said Sundays are the busiest, all afternoon and until dawn. Your free day will be in the middle of the week."

Little Grandfather placed his hands palms down on the table and leaned forward. "I knew something bad would happen yesterday. The breeze felt unnatural, and a huge iguana waddled across the front yard. It looked around a long time. And on a Friday."

Isabela cried softly all night, thinking of her father's death and about what awaited her.

Isabela had lain with a few of the boys from the village, and she enjoyed the act well enough. Her girlfriends told her she would grow to love it. But the idea of performing it with strangers repulsed her. She disagreed with her mother's comment that she would get used to it. And now as predawn light filled the Ortega home her first thought became a hope that none of the men from San Lucas would find her in her new capacity at one of those houses.

Isabela looked at her sisters sleeping on each side of her on the mat they shared. *Yes. They're too young. And I shouldn't have to do this either. But Papa's gone now. As Little Grandfather said, there is no other remedy.* Isabela, always one of the first to rise, felt burdened this morning, oppressed by sadness about her father, by fear of the unknown, and by dread.

She listened to her mother preparing breakfast, heard her grandfather rise, cough, greet Isabela's mother in the kitchen, and open and close the front door on his way to the outhouse. Her sisters stirred. Her brothers, sharing a mat on the other side of the room, started talking and giggling. *Do they understand what I'll be doing? Do my sisters? I hope not.* She rose to help her mother.

"Mama, is Maritza the only one from San Lucas to work in one of the houses?"

"There are probably a couple of others. No one talks openly. But there's gossip. Villages like ours always provide some girls."

"I wish I didn't have to be one of them."

"So do I. But—"

"I know, Mama. It's bad enough losing Papa. You feel awful too."

Her mother nodded, pinched off enough from the ball of corn dough for a tortilla.

Isabela said, "I cried all night for Papa . . . and for myself."

"I know. I heard you. So did I."

"I considered running away. But I didn't know where to go. And I don't want to disappoint you and Little Grandfather."

Isabela pinched off some dough, made a ball, and began patting it flat, soon tossing it from hand to hand, then onto the grill. "I hope my Spanish is good enough."

"You'll do well. I've heard you talking to your friends and practicing with your brothers and sisters, even though I didn't understand much."

"But everyone will know I'm Huichol."

"Yes, and you'll be the prettiest girl there."

Isabela's hair, black and satiny, had seldom been trimmed, draped to the small of her back. Her teeth, well formed, put coconut meat to shame. Large round eyes, black like her hair, spoke of honesty, loyalty, and intelligence. Though she had blocky fingers with short nails and ragged cuticles, she knew they could be improved. "I just hope I won't be the only Indian."

"Probably not. And you'll need shoes right away. Your huaraches won't do."

"Why will I need shoes?"

"Everyone wears them. To be dressy, more formal, and appealing, I suppose."

"How do I get them?"

"The duenna will probably have some extras. If not, she'll send you into town with other girls. She'll take it out of your pay. Get a new dress or two also."

"Won't shoes make me walk drunk?"

"Just at first. You'll become accustomed to them."

Isabela liked the thought of having money, though not the way she had to earn it. "I hope the others are nice and don't steal my money."

"They won't have a chance. Customers pay the duenna. They say she keeps a ledger and credits each girl with half of their earnings. When you need money she'll give you some and keep track. You should keep track too. Maritza said the girls can go into town almost any morning if they dress nice and behave. They'll give you a new name too for dealing with men."

"I want to buy ice cream and a *Chanoc* comic book."

"You'll get to learn a little English too, from tourists. That should be enough tortillas. Want to pour the coffee?"

"Yes, Mama. For the last time."

"Don't make me feel any worse." She used the back of her hand to wipe away a tear. "If you knew about life in a big city you could do such work there and return home and no one would know. But you'll be safer and more comfortable down the mountain. And it's easier to come home from time to time."

"I hope none of the men from our village find me there. I don't want to have to move away like Maritza."

"Probably that won't happen. And lots of wealthy men from Guadalajara and elsewhere vacation in the town for the boating and fishing and sunshine. Sometimes a good man meets a young woman in one of the houses and carries her away."

"You mean kidnap them like Pancho Villa in the Revolution?"

"No, I mean set them up fancy in the city. Maybe they marry if the girl is young and pretty. No one else ever knows her past."

"Could that happen to me?"

"Maybe."

"I would miss you and everyone."

"You'd have so much money. You send for us to visit you and your new family at your grand winter home on the beach in Acapulco."

Isabela laughed, then sobbed.

Her mother hugged her. "Go get your sisters and brothers."

"Maybe we could all move when I come back."

"But this is our home."

Crying softly, Isabela went to rouse her siblings.

Packing after breakfast did not take long. Isabela knelt on the smooth dirt floor beside her sleeping mat, spread her red mantilla, and placed her huaraches and change of under-clothing on it first. A well-worn magazine of soap opera plots and actors' biographies followed her Spanish grammar, three comic books, comb, brush, hair ribbons, and tooth-brush. She added a small cloth purse and her Sunday dress, both sewn by her mother.

In a chapel veil Isabela had seldom worn she wrapped the eagle's wing tip, the jaguar tooth, and—a gift from her father long ago—a small wooden crucifix. She laid them on top. *I could have placed those items in the purse. Too late. So what?*

Isabela gave her remaining comic books and maga-zine photo of Ricky Martin to her sisters but folded up and placed into her dress pocket her similar photo of an art-ist's depiction of Cuauhtémoc. With the back of her hand she wiped her tears. She sat on her heels and sighed, finally inhaled deeply. She drew the ends of the mantilla together, tied them, and stood.

"I'll escort you, Isabelita. I can do that much." Little Grandfather waited in the front yard. He held ropes looped around the heads and muzzles of two burros, the black one slightly larger than the other, a more common gray.

"Do I get to ride Porfirio?" Isabela pointed to the gray. "He has such a nice gait."

"Of course. Did you tell your brothers and sisters good-bye?"

She nodded. "They asked a lot of questions, but I told them I'd visit soon and explain everything. They went back to their games."

"Isabela," her mother called from the open door. "Did you forget anything?"

"No, Mama." She held her bundle up for her mother to see, lowered it, and joined her in the doorway. They hugged and kissed. Isabela turned and hurried to Porfirio, leaping onto his back despite her long dress.

The rain-cleaned air invigorated her. The soil had absorbed the night's moisture.

Beside her grandfather astride the bigger Cortés, black and fidgeting, she waved to her mother, tried to smile, couldn't, fought to hold back tears, and couldn't. Isabela and Little Grandfather started down the mountain.

She hadn't ridden so much in a long time, felt relieved upon seeing rooftops and the church tower through the pines and chicle trees, the bananas and coconuts and mangos, the bay their background. "Little Grandfather, let's walk. I'm getting stiff and sore."

"Go ahead. We'll be there soon."

Isabela dismounted holding her bundle, patted Porfirio's neck. "How will we know which are the houses?"

"I'll know."

"But how? Are there signs?"

"No signs."

"Then how—?"

"Just never you mind."

Isabela realized she should change the subject. "Will the town have a shaman?"

"Just a priest."

"Once a month like in San Lucas?"

"All the time. But don't go to him." He pointed. "There they are." He stopped Cortés beside Isabela, who examined the three whitewashed-and-stuccoed buildings in a cluster, the middle one of two stories, the others of one. Red tiles roofed them. Palms and banana trees fought with prickly pear cactus for attention along drab exteriors.

"Why are they way out here instead of more in the town?"

"It's the custom. We go to the middle one. The duenna should be there."

Isabela, sobbing silently with each step, cradled her bundle, led Porfirio by the rope around his muzzle.

Near the front door they stopped, and Little Grandfather, grunting with discomfort, dismounted and hitched the burros to a post. "Come on."

Isabela swallowed a sob, shifted her belongings, and stepped forward. The crucifix slipped from her bundle and fell into the dirt. She didn't notice.

The duenna showed Isabela to a cubicle and filled her mind with so many instructions and tips that Isabela's head spun, a leaf in a whirlpool, hurt like the woman had smacked her with a coconut. After the duenna left, the girl sat on the narrow bed and opened her bundle. She hung up her Sunday dress and placed her huaraches beside the bed.

Isabela lay on her back on the bed. She sighed. *I wonder what my sisters and brothers are doing. And my mother. I hope Little Grandfather gets home safely.* She turned onto her side and examined the near wall, considered where her picture of Cuauhtémoc might look good. *I hope I don't have any customers tonight. Oops. The duenna said refer to them as clients. Either way I'm so tired from riding that burro. I just want to rest.*

Isabela felt saddened when she realized she had lost the crucifix her father gave her. But the eagle's wing tip and the jaguar's beautiful tooth consoled her.

Catalina

◇◇◇◇◇◇◇◇◇◇◇◇◇◇

"Listen, beloved and highly respected husband, brave and handsome hero of our valley," Mama yelled, "the next time your garbage machine of a burro gnaws on my flowers, I will, in the names of Jesús, María, and José, shoot her."

"Well, my long-pursued and ever-cherished wife and sweetheart," my father shouted, "prettiest and most-desired treasure of all Jalisco, the next time that uninhibited flirt of yours skips through my cornfield counter to the rows, I will be the executioner, and I will be justified."

That's how Mama and Papa reacted to the slightest little thing Catalina did that displeased them, always blaming each other, electrifiable. When Catalina nibbled the flowers or unavoidably strolled through Mama's vegetable garden, she belonged to Papa. When Catalina relaxed in the irrigation ditch, blocking the water's flow, or ate immature cornstalks, maybe mashing others as she innocently walked somewhere, Mama owned her.

The fact is Catalina belonged to me. Papa paid for her, and he never gave her to me. But I got to name her, choosing the saint's day she arrived. And I could claim Catalina because we communicated. I'm not saying we talked to one another. I was only ten, but I knew better than that. It's that Catalina and I knew each other's habits and faults, what the other enjoyed doing, and we wanted to please one another. Lots of dogs are that way, and some horses, and occasionally even people. But the characteristic is uncommon in burros. It made Catalina such a rare and wonderful friend.

Papa and Mama never believed Catalina and I could communicate, though they recognized her special qualities. They even say they loved her. But in the beginning I know they didn't understand or fully appreciate Catalina.

Like the first time she entered our home with me. I'm sure Catalina felt natural and good following me. The floor of our adobe house is dirt packed hard and swept clean. When she walked onto my sleeping mat I saw that as no different from my walking on it. We even smelled alike, according to Mama, because we spent so much time together.

I told Mama I would pick up any droppings right away. But she got instantly angry. A few minutes later when Papa returned from the fields and saw Catalina inside he got upset too.

"I'm going to sell her or trade her in the morning," Papa said.

"Why wait?" Mama told him.

This didn't become the first time they said something similar, but they had never agreed simultaneously on a solution. I put my arm around Catalina's neck and hurried her out.

Catalina was grown but still young when Papa acquired her to carry firewood for us to burn or peddle or corn to sell in the village. And fortunately I got to ride her because I couldn't handle our mule.

She settled in with us right away, like she'd never had a family and wanted one, specifically us. Catalina had a mostly gray hide, the pale, almost foggy shade of first light in our valley. Her tail and spine carried numerous strands of black, and a great deal of white splashed her undersides and throat and the edges of her ears. A creamy shade of white around her eyes and muzzle didn't make her look old like it did so many burros. She had the strength of a burro twice her size, and she toiled enthusiastically because she enjoyed being around people.

"I've never heard of a burro working as well as this one," Papa often said.

When our mule went lame for a few weeks, and later when it had the colic, Papa plowed with Catalina. Mostly, however, I handled her. I'd take her to gather firewood, which I'd tie onto her back, and I'd walk her to the river with cans for water, or with different cans to the neighbor's. They owned a cow and we bought milk when they had it on the same day we could afford it or brought something to trade. Papa had made a wooden rack to fit Catalina's back so I could attach the cans to it.

As another of her peccadilloes—one of Papa's words— Catalina often trotted down the trail to the road and explored along the road itself, staying gone for hours, being no use at all to us. And on occasions she wanted to play instead of work, and we had to handle her with special patience. But she never acted mulish like some burros.

"Segundo, everything is play to that little varmint," Mama used to tell me.

Perhaps. Maybe she never grew up.

I did most of the riding, but Papa or Mama also straddled her if either needed to go someplace the bus didn't or if not wanting to wait for the bus, which didn't pass often or regularly. We rode bareback.

Of course when Catalina toted a load I walked. But I didn't follow behind, switching her from time to time and clucking and giving orders the way some men do. I walked right beside her, sometimes with my arm around her neck, sometimes rubbing her ears. Catalina preferred to work that way. If I wandered off to climb a rock and look around or strayed to hunt for snakes or lizards she stopped and waited for me, giving me a patient, protective look. Papa and Mama didn't believe that any more than they believed she loved them almost as much as she loved me.

I cried the first time Papa sold her.

"Segundo," he said, "I don't have any choice. She's just too destructive."

"But Papa—"

"Child, she also plays around too much, makes me forget her good qualities."

I started to remind Papa of Catalina's good qualities, but he wouldn't listen. So he helped put her into the buyer's trailer, and the man drove off.

Catalina returned the next day. She had broken the rope fettering her and walked and trotted half the night cross-country and through our valley, arriving by way of Papa's cornfield shortly after breakfast with the rope still tied to her right-front leg and Catalina chewing on the torn end.

The new owner—I suppose I should say "previous owner"—drove up while I brushed Catalina. I quickly led her behind the house and told her how glad I felt to see her.

"Absolutely not," the man said when Papa offered to again help put Catalina into his trailer. "There's another burro for sale down the road. Just give me my money back."

"But what did she do?" Papa's voice seemed falsely tinged of innocence.

"She brayed all the rest of the day and into the night. We couldn't sleep. She finally shut up but we didn't realize until dawn that our pitifully few hours of rest owed themselves to her having run off. As she escaped she trampled my newly planted bean field."

So I cried that day too, this time with happiness, and that night we slept side by side under the big tree on the hill behind our house. That tree became special to me and her. It didn't give fruit and not much shade. What it furnished that could be seen were beautiful flowers. What could not be seen were its strength and peace and companionship. And it taught tolerance and understanding, patience and love.

"I suppose you slept with the burro," Mama said the next morning.

"It's what Catalina wanted."

Mama shrugged and continued making tortillas for breakfast.

When the blooms opened fully they were golden, about as big as Papa's fist, with eight or ten large petals and sweet little edible shoots inside. Catalina and I enjoyed the shoots, which I picked for her. After a few days the blooms turned red. I wish I could think of the tree's name.

Catalina often went alone to that wonderful tree. The branches started high up the trunk, though I don't think she would have chewed on its flowers even if she could have reached them. But Catalina liked to rub her rump or ribs or neck on the trunk or lie beside it and twitch her ears while watching our home or the valley. If she hungered for flowers she ate Mama's.

When neither of us had chores we sometimes went into the hills to explore. I didn't use rope or reins, guiding her with my knees and heels. Other times I walked beside her, patting her neck and talking to her. Catalina seemed to know where I wanted to go.

A refreshing spring and lots of trees and good views are in that direction, although it's not true that from those hills you can see all the way to Guadalajara.

On Sunday mornings I would find cornstalk leaves or a small green branch from an olive tree close to the house, tie the leaves or branch between Catalina's ears, and ride her to the church in the village. If Mama weren't watching I used a rose from her garden instead.

On Sunday afternoons Catalina went with me to a field some of us had cleared of rocks, and she watched while we ran and fell down and kicked a ball or bounced it off our heads or legs or shoulders. Occasionally she trotted through our playing field, usually at a crucial moment. This would cause some of the other boys to yell at her, nasty words I'd never heard Papa say. However, I never let them throw rocks or sticks at her, just soft clods at her rump. After all, it was only a game and she merely wanted to cross to the other side.

When Catalina lay in our irrigation ditch to refresh herself for a third consecutive day she blocked it worse than ever. Papa grabbed a shovel and ran to the destroyed area to try to stop the water from being wasted or flooding the wrong places.

"Grab a shovel, Segundo. She's done it this time."

Mama used a hoe to help. It took a lot of work and time. Papa praised me for my contribution. Then he upset me.

"I'm selling that pest again," Papa said. "Or giving her away."

My protests went unheeded.

When a new purchaser arrived Papa told him of the trouble Catalina caused the first time he sold her. "Maybe you should pen her up in a corral."

"Not necessary," the man said. "I have several burros for my business. They have the herd instinct. This Catalina will stay with the others near the feed and water. Have a cigar."

"What is that business?" Papa accepted the cigar.

"Hauling smooth rounded stones from the Cuale River and its banks and taking them into town. The mayor is building cobblestone streets. I have a big contract and must complete the work on time to get a bonus."

Papa looked at me over his cigar.

I couldn't read his expression. And I couldn't keep quiet. "Catalina is going to haul rocks all day?"

"Of course," the man said. "She's young and strong, just the animal I need."

"But she's not a—She's a . . . poet. Yes. A poet."

The man laughed.

Papa gave me a helpless look, like the time the biggest fish we'd ever caught broke his line and swam away downstream.

"That's top price I offer," the man said. "Is it a deal?"

Papa nodded slowly, didn't look at me.

I ran inside and cried, though not as long as before. I knew Catalina had more pet instinct than herd instinct.

That night I had trouble getting to sleep. But I finally dozed some. Around what must have been midnight her braying awoke me. I could tell it came from the hill with the tree whose flowers turned from yellow to red. I'm sure I smiled as I went back to sleep.

"I give up," Papa said in the morning. He looked out the window.

Mama and I saw what he saw: Catalina trotting down the hill to us. Mama put her arm around me.

Catalina's bray didn't resemble others in our part of the valley. It started with a wheezing, gasping hee-haw and ended several seconds later the same way but with a snort. She brayed when angry, happy, or frustrated, and always at dawn, when I suspect she felt happiest.

Right after Papa acquired her she introduced us to her bray because Papa fettered her. The shackling didn't last long. So Papa assigned her to the mule corral. It held her in but unleashed her bray. He couldn't fence the whole cornfield or irrigation ditch, so he had to tolerate her wanderings. Mama figured Catalina would knock down any fence around her flowers, so she made me promise to keep Catalina out of them. Catalina seemed to understand, because she nibbled around the edges only and backed away when I told her to.

If Catalina had been a man she could have been elected president. Among people praising her even today are a half-dozen field workers from our neighboring villages. They had cut sugar cane all day on land of one of the big owners, and the foreman began driving them in a pickup truck toward their homes, letting them off singly or in pairs at the edge of the road near paths to their villages. Several more men rode in the truck earlier but had left it by the time Catalina entered the lives of the half-dozen.

Nowadays when people from our valley tell the story that little pickup truck has sometimes grown into a thirty-passenger bus and the six men are fifty. And many a man who only heard about what happened claims with pride and sincerity that he had been in the bed of that truck, asserts he tingled with the sweat of fright, said his prayers, trembled, saw the driver squeezing the steering wheel, mashing the brake pedal, jerking on the hand brake while the truck careened down the hill.

I figured out later that while the truck rolled hell-bent for the edge of the Earth, Catalina had been enjoying one of her frequent wanderings. Trotting downhill, she had nearly reached the trail to our village when the pickup struck her from behind.

"That little creature got in our way on purpose," one of the survivors told Papa. "She crossed the road at the last minute. The driver couldn't stop. We were racing like the Devil fleeing the Madonna. We'd have never made the curve, would have sailed off the road into the arroyo." He paused and nodded real fast three times. "We'd have all been killed if not for her."

But Catalina's entanglement with the truck's wheels and undercarriage caused it to slow down, skid, and stop. It teetered on the edge of the curve, on the lip of the slope.

The rich man who owned the truck and had hired the workers arranged to have Catalina brought in. Papa and Mama thanked him, told how important Catalina had been to all of us. Hearing that proved to me that Papa and Mama cared for Catalina, though they had never let on. And I quit crying long enough to address him.

"Mister, could you have your workers take Catalina up yonder?" I pointed.

"No, Segundo," Papa said. "The gentleman has gone out of his way to do this much."

"But that's where Catalina and I used to go to rest and think and look over the valley."

Papa shook his head, smiled at the man.

But the gentleman placed his hand on my shoulder. "After what the little animal did for us? Of course." He also gave Papa money, which Papa refused until Mama poked his back.

Crying all the while, I buried her under that tree. The next day on our front steps I began carving a marker for her grave. I struggled with it so I took a break and walked to the site of the accident, where I built a shrine on the curve. That also took a lot of work, and I'm proud of it: two feet high and a foot wide on each side with a window, stones cemented together with lime and water except for one rock the size of my fist. That one I can remove to light the candle in front of the little wooden cross I set there. And it permits me to leave offerings, usually an ear of corn or a tortilla or some of Mama's flowers.

A few days later I realized that my difficulty in carving the grave marker for Catalina owed to my working on it at home. So I took my pocket knife and the wood and once more climbed the hill to her grave and the tree that flowered red and gold.

This time, in Catalina's company, with the flowers protecting us and Catalina's presence inspiring me, the work went well. First I carved the date she came to us and when she left. I considered adding what happened to her, how she'd saved the men's lives and how brave she'd been, how wonderful, and how we loved her, the grand walks she and I took, the humorous things Catalina did. But the marker would have to be much larger. And after I'd thought a while I realized I didn't need all that information, that her full name would say it all.

I ran to Papa in the cornfield, where he plowed with the mule. He liked my idea.

I hurried into the house to tell Mama. She began crying and nodding.

So I ran back up the hill and finished that marker when I carved, "Saint Catalina."

THE GOOD GUY

Federico Ponce came to the town from the mountain village of San Miguel. Nowadays few people in the town
know even that about him.

He had been born and raised in San Miguel and for several years had grown corn on the slopes there, the same as his
people before him. He owned pigs and chickens, two goats,
a milk cow, and two burros, both rideable, one suitable for
plowing. Federico worked hard, saved his money, did not go
to the cantina nor gamble on the cockfights.

The villagers respected him, liked him, knew Federico to
be among their wealthiest citizens.

Following his burros loaded with corn, he had occasionally descended the mountain to the rim of the great bay
that opened up to the endless ocean. So he had seen the
town, heard of jobs not requiring toil from dawn to dusk
except for Sunday afternoon like in San Miguel. And Federico Ponce began to wonder if his arduous life and those of
his wife and children must forever be fettered on the slopes
of that mountain.

"In the town," Federico said one evening, "there are
other kinds of work."

"We don't know any other kinds," his wife said.

"Teresa, we're still young. We could learn."

"We don't know anyone there."

"We will meet them."

"But you're too timid. Here that doesn't matter. We know everyone."

"Teresa, you are too pretty to be stuck here as though tied to a tree."

"I like it here. I like us here."

"We will like it more in the town. The children will have better schools. There is even a motion picture theater. We can sell the livestock for a stake and lease our land."

"I'm scared."

"We'll be all right."

They talked far into the night.

In and around Puerto Vallarta, where groves of bananas and coconuts are plentiful and fish bountiful, a man's stomach seldom suffers. Also, visitors from Guadalajara and other lands stop by to enjoy the fine weather, to swim and fish and acquire suntans. They purchase pretty shirts and embroidered dresses and broad-brimmed straw hats, short pants and huaraches and souvenirs. They eat a lot. And they help the cantinas prosper.

Work to serve the visitors and create items for them is usually available. But because of Federico's shyness, ignorance, and being provincial he couldn't find a job as waiter or salesman or clerk. He decided on fishing, honorable employment not as demanding as farming.

When he failed to locate an affordable used boat he commissioned construction of a large canoe from an elephant ear tree in the hills. While the boat makers toiled, Federico loitered around the dock and the beaches to capture knowledge about boats and their motors and fishing. His reticence prevented him from asking as many questions as he wanted. But he also learned by observation.

And one day on the pier Federico met Juan Feliz.

Federico had noticed the handsome fishing boat because of the passengers singing *Cielito Lindo*. He watched the vessel motor slowly, round the pier, and stop at a cleat opposite him. When a crewman tossed a line that landed near the cleat, Federico knew from his observations he should as a courtesy weave the rope in a figure eight around the cleat. So he did that.

The singing diminished. Passengers laughing and smiling stepped onto the pier, and some moved toward a sign Federico hadn't paid attention to: "Fish With Johnny. No Fish, No Pay." Crewmen unloaded strings of fish large and small. Singly and in groups the passengers posed with the fish and photographed one another under the sign. They also urged one of the crew to pose with them.

"Come on, Johnny," several said, and a man left the boat to stand under the sign with the others. Federico saw how happily the passengers grabbed the man, called him Johnny, and took turns standing close to him. He wore swimsuit, huaraches, and a captain's hat. A medallion hung around his neck.

After having their pictures taken, two women shook Johnny's hand and left, passing near Federico, who stepped aside to watch and listen, though he didn't expect to understand.

"What a physique," the blonde said.

"Yummy." The brunette licked her lips.

"With that crooked grin, the thin mustache, and those laughing eyes, he could be the new Clark Gable if he can act. Somebody should get him to Hollywood."

"I don't care if he can act," the other said. "I'd just like to get him."

They laughed and swayed into one another.

Federico turned at the approach of the young man who had posed for pictures with the visitors, wondered why he stopped in front of him.

"I saw how you helped tie up my boat," the young man said.

Federico tensed.

The boat owner extended his hand and smiled. "Thank you. I'm Juan Feliz."

Federico relaxed, accepted his hand, introduced himself.

"Do you fish?" Juan Feliz said.

"I'm having a boat made. Then I will."

"Good. Let me know when you're ready. I'll point out some good spots for you—fishing, diving, sightseeing." Juan pointed to his sign. "That's me."

"But why does your sign say 'Johnny'?"

"American tourists like to give us their version of our names."

"Must I learn the English?"

"That would help a lot."

"I see. I heard two of your passengers talking, but I caught only one word clearly. Juan, what is a clarkgable?"

"Who knows? I speak the English but not all of it. They baffle me too."

Federico told Teresa about meeting Juan. "He's going to help me get started."

She looked up from her sewing in the back of the dress shop, where she had easily found employment, for she always made clothes for herself and family. "I hear about him a lot. Very popular. He's called Johnny Feliz. They say he's a good guy."

Every afternoon Federico watched for Juan's boat to return. He could hear the singing as it neared the pier, and he watched the laughing, chatting passengers disembark and pose for pictures under Johnny's sign. When the passengers had left, Federico helped Johnny and his crewmen—tall muscular Eulogio and small wiry Santos—load the catch of fish into sacks for carrying to the hotels. He also helped collect the empty beer cans and swab the deck.

"My crew does that," Johnny told him.

"I like to help, and I'm learning things." Federico's attire had become swimsuit, huaraches, and a captain's hat. A St. Christopher's medallion hung around his neck. "Why is *Carmelita* painted on the end of your boat?"

"The stern. It's her name. Most boats are female. Carmelita is my wife."

"Should all boats be named for wives?"

"It's a good idea."

Johnny gave Federico other advice. "If they want red snapper, take them over there." He pointed to a distant bend in the great bay. "If they want mackerel, you go over there." He pointed. "Oysters find themselves on rocks at Los Cochinos. I show you.

"Swimmers like to see coral. The best growths are at Bucerías." He gestured. "A little town is kind of hidden there. Tourists like hidden places. But if they swim near coral they should wear tennis shoes to avoid cuts when they walk into or out of the water."

"What about sharks?"

"All kinds. I've seen some huge ones too. But they're usually far out in the deep and don't often bother swimmers. Sharks are mainly interested in schools of small fish."

"I've heard about manta rays."

"They are big and scary, but they don't bite or sting."

Federico laughed. "I will stay in my boat."

A week later Federico had been watching activities on the beach and pier for much of the afternoon when a mule arrived dragging the big canoe that had been the trunk of an elephant ear tree. Two men in straw hats and denims completed the team.

"This took lots of work," the taller of the muleteers said.

"I'm sure." Federico withdrew several bills from his wallet and offered them to the taller man. "Thank you both very much. It's beautiful."

The man squeezed the bills but left his hand extended. "More."

"You have the amount we agreed on."

"The job took too long. I had to hire extra men and rent the mule."

Federico knew this couldn't be fair. No one on the mountain would act this way. Anyone who did might find his body parts rearranged by the slash of a machete. But in a large town like this . . . And Federico . . . *I don't know what to tell this man.* He felt himself shrink beneath the muleteer's scowl. And he paid the other's demand.

Later that day while Federico walked around his boat and wondered how he'd launch it by himself, Juan Feliz joined him.

"I made a mistake, Juan. I won't be able to row this with people in it, even if I learn how to float it."

Johnny Feliz laughed and put his arm around Federico. "You need only two things. I get them for you."

The used engine he located for Federico did not cost much.

"It will run until the century plant blooms twice," Juan assured him, and he helped Federico attach it to the stern and told him where to buy gasoline in a can. "When you want to put your canoe into the water, any boy loafing on the beach will help for a few centavos. Same for beaching it at the end of the day. Now: boards for seats."

Juan located the necessary materials, brought his tools, and helped Federico create the seats. "Now you need a sign like I have. Do you know any of the English?"

"Just 'clarkgable.' And I still don't know what it means. But Teresa has learned some at the dress shop. And she has a dictionary. I can do it, Juan. You've done enough."

The next day Juan stopped by the spot Federico chose at the lap of the bay. He moaned when he saw Federico finishing his sign: "Canoe To Rent Itself." Juan asked Federico for the brush and paint.

"Isn't my sign good?"

"Not the best, my friend." When Juan finished, the sign said: "Fish With Freddie. No Fish, No Pay." Juan told him what the English said.

"What's a 'Freddie'?"

"That's you. Easier for tourists to say."

Few people sailed with Federico at first. But when he learned to buy a bucket of minnows early each day at the nearby bait shack, and as he slowly gained a modest vocabulary in English, his customer count grew, and he obtained discounts for them when they rented tackle. Johnny Feliz told him where to take a customer's fish to be frozen until the tourist prepared to leave on his return flight, and on Juan's advice Federico accepted US dollars as well as Mexican pesos. He worked hard and he saved money.

Federico knew he couldn't be like Juan, leading the clients in song and joking with them. But he felt his customers liked him. When at Juan's suggestion Federico started providing cans of beer in an ice chest he felt they liked him more. He mentioned that to Juan.

"Of course. They feel like it's free because they don't pay separately for it." Juan also told his friend to not flirt with the women, even those unescorted. "That can cause trouble."

"No, Teresa wouldn't like it."

"That too."

One day Juan urged Federico to acquire a regular fishing boat. "Carry more people and make more money."

"How would I pay for it?"

"Get a used one. Not too big but modern. Pay in

installments. I can help. You'll be able to pay me back quicker than you can sing *La Cucaracha*."

Juan helped him sell his canoe and acquire a boat smaller than his but a seaworthy bargain. Federico cleaned it and painted Teresa's name on the stern. Juan helped him move his sign to the pier.

"But what if people see my sign and fish with me instead of you?"

Juan laughed and placed his arm around Federico. "It's a large bay, my friend. Beyond the points is a vast ocean. And we have more visitors every year."

"But I don't want you to see me as a barnacle on your boat."

Juan Feliz laughed again, hugged Federico, and moved away to meet customers waiting.

That winter the town attracted more visitors than ever. Many wanted to fish, to dive, to swim in isolated coves, and visit villages hidden by coconut palms and banana trees. The tourists kept the fishing boats busy, none as much as Johnny Feliz's, though the man they called Freddie with the boat named *Teresa* also prospered.

Federico moved his wife and children to a larger home closer to the center of town, to schools, and the church. Teresa enjoyed a much shorter walk to the dress shop, Federico to the pier.

"I'm so pleased with our new life," Teresa said one day at breakfast.

"Me too," Federico said. "I want to fish forever."

"We owe so much to Juan."

"Yes. And not just the money he loaned us but in all ways."

"I know," Teresa said. "Everyone knows."

"'Everyone'?"

"This is a small town. He has helped others. Juan could be mayor if he wanted."

Federico knew he could never be so popular. But he would do his best to be like Juan. He would try to be the other good guy.

Even more visitors arrived the following year.

"I need your help," Juan said when they met on the pier.

Federico felt pleased and flattered.

"There's a large group on vacation here, men with their wives. They want to cruise around the bay for a while, maybe go swimming."

"But how could I help?"

"My boat can't hold them all. I'd like for you to take some."

"You could make two trips. Or one today and one tomorrow."

"No. Tomorrow they have a big meeting planned at their hotel. The next day they take the boat up the river to the jungle. Everything is scheduled. Then they leave."

Federico had never taken a vacation, but he had heard talk, though not about so strictly programming one.

"I'd better get lots of minnows."

"No. I asked about fishing. They said 'hang the fish.' I'm not sure what that means, except they don't want to fish."

Federico shook his head, smiled feebly.

"They wear funny hats and they do everything together. They're called Shriners."

Federico shrugged. "Tell me how to help."

The overflow from Juan's boat filled Federico's to the gunwales. If the *Teresa* had been much smaller, the last Shriners and their wives would not have fitted. The men wore funny hats, and several men and women wore swimsuits.

"We'll go slow," Juan said. "Let's keep together so the men and women can talk from boat to boat easily and toss beer cans back and forth. They like to do that."

"I've never heard of such people."

"Shriners have been here before. Not this group, but from other American cities."

They motored almost gunwale to gunwale, slowly and near the shoreline, first to Playa de Oro, so the Shriners could see what their hotel looked like from the water. Then Juan and Federico put their vessels into a large loop and went south so the visitors could view the entire town and the verdant ascent connecting to Guadalajara.

Juan talked across the rail to Federico while his crewman Eulogio steered. "We'll tie up to the small pier at Mismaloya. They can walk to the little houses the Hollywood people built several years ago for a movie about iguanas. Then we'll go across the bay to a cove with a large beach that's shaded this time of day. Shriners sunburn easily."

"They sure drink a lot."

"It's a big part of their vacation. But in their city they work hard. Some are ordinary men like us. Others are doctors and lawyers and scientists. When they become Shriners, however, they are all equal."

Many of the Shriners and their wives sat on the sand with an ice chest full of beer in the shade of coconut palms. Some set their hats in a row on the sand and swam in the cove, which lacked coral. Others sat in shallow water. Away from the group, Eulogio and Santos kicked a soccer ball back and forth. Johnny and Federico sat near their boats, anchored in shallow water.

"What do you think of the Shriners, Federico?"

"I don't know."

"Yes you do. Tell me."

"They're awfully noisy. I suppose I don't understand them."

"What else?"

"Well . . . on the mountain we had pulque and our own liquor, *raicilla*. Made them ourselves and enjoyed fiestas. But I've never heard of revelry like this."

"It's common, Federico."

"Especially I've never seen women drink the same as men."

Loud laughter exploded from a red-haired woman in the group on the sand.

"Another thing." Federico nodded in her direction. "She smiles at me too much."

Juan Feliz laughed softly. "It's all right to not like them."

"But I want to, Juan."

"Let me tell you something that could help."

Federico waited.

"When I was ten or twelve," Juan said, "a little kid in town was horribly bent and twisted. He couldn't stand, could hardly sit, just scooted around, begging, though everyone said his mother lived and worked here somewhere. I suppose some people knew her. We all felt sorry for the boy. But what could we do? He'd been born that way. We called him The Broken-Back Kid.

"One day when a Shriners meeting like this one came to town, my father, who waited table at their hotel, heard a couple of them talking. They spoke Spanish with a funny accent, like they grew up in Texas or California. But my father understood. One was a doctor. My father heard him tell the other, 'My colleagues can fix that broken-back kid.' And the other said, 'Let's do it.'"

"They operated?"

"They sent him to a children's hospital in California, surgery and rehabilitation." Juan nodded toward Eulogio and Santos. "You know them."

"Yes."

"The big strong one? Eulogio? You have seen the scar on his back?"

"Once when he'd taken his T-shirt off. I couldn't ask how he got it."

"No, not you." Juan nodded at Eulogio. "He used to be The Broken-Back Kid."

Johnny Feliz led them diagonally toward the pier instead of along the shoreline. "We've been out long enough. We need to save time."

"Suits me, Juan."

Something else suited Federico: The woman who smiled too much at him had led her husband to Juan's boat for the return trip. They needed help, like others, to climb onto Juan's boat, while a different couple filled their spot on Federico's. On both vessels the singing started immediately, and conversations across the railings resumed.

Juan set a faster pace on the way home. *Yes,* Federico observed, *he is also in a hurry to complete this expedition.*

Federico occasionally glanced at the passengers on the *Carmelita,* saw Juan had handed the wheel to Eulogio and mingled, laughing and talking. When the woman who smiled too much moved close to Juan, he smiled and spoke, and stepped away.

Federico looked at the sea and nodded. A few minutes later when Federico once more glanced at his friend's boat, he didn't see the woman who had seemed to pursue Juan. Eulogio continued to steer, and Juan still mingled. *I couldn't do that even if I had someone to relieve me at the wheel. Juan is special.*

The boats, hulls again almost touching, had neared the halfway point when Federico heard a shout and saw the *Carmelita* veer away. Federico puzzled about the maneuver. He saw Juan, teeth clamped onto a knife, kick off his huaraches and dive into the water.

And in the distance Federico saw someone swimming poorly and waving frantically. *Had too much to drink, I'll bet, and fell overboard.*

Federico drew the *Teresa* alongside Juan's boat. They completed a loop and began retracing their wakes, soon heading for the swimmer, still moving poorly, now also crying for help. Because of the wide turn the boats had to make, Federico realized that Juan would reach the swimmer before either vessel.

Federico heard the *Carmelita*'s engine slowing. He reduced the *Teresa*'s speed.

And Federico recognized the swimmer: the red-haired woman who smiled too much. Federico heard shouting, distinguished one of the first words he'd learned in English.

"Shark!" everyone seemed to shout. "Shark!"

Federico scanned the bay around and behind the woman, couldn't see any danger, and then he did: A large dorsal fin circled the woman and disappeared.

When Juan reached her the Shriners and their wives cheered. After he warded off her flailing arms, turned her around, and began towing her toward his boat, they urged him on.

The boats drifted toward the swimmers. Federico again saw the dorsal fin, ominous, scary, slicing through the water as though carving a circle around Juan and the woman. Again he watched it disappear.

"Hurry, Johnny," Federico heard several shout.

Juan, so close Federico could almost touch him, pushed the woman into helping hands. And he heard the observers cheer louder and more enthusiastically. Federico also felt like cheering.

When the woman reached the deck and collapsed, several reached out to pull Juan onto the boat.

This time Federico could see the entire shark.

It grasped Juan's legs and carried him away.

For three days everyone with a boat cruised Banderas Bay and scrutinized beaches, hoping to find Juan Feliz safely washed ashore. Then the mayor declared him dead, lowered the City Hall flag to half-mast, and decreed a week of mourning.

A funeral Mass at the church drew the largest crowd old-timers had ever seen there. A second ceremony took place in the cemetery at a cenotaph the mayor had ordered for Juan. Federico, Teresa, and their children stood in the back at both services.

"Juan was such a good guy," several mourners said.

From Eulogio, the mayor obtained Juan's huaraches. He had them bronzed, mounted on a plaque, and the plaque affixed to the City Hall façade beside the entry.

Federico, Teresa, and their children stood in the back at the plaque ceremony.

A wealthy Mexico City industrialist with a winter home on the rim of the bay commissioned a life-size bronze of Juan for the town square.

When the week of mourning ended, Federico, sad and out of sorts, returned to work. Tall strong Eulogio and small wiry Santos, with the blessing of Juan's widow, operated the *Carmelita* from the "Fish With Johnny" sign on the pier. Nearby, Federico loaded clients onto the *Teresa* from his "Fish with Freddie" sign.

The new crop of tourists that winter mistook Eulogio for Johnny. That distressed Federico, but he kept working, for business thrived.

Some tourists hired Federico's boat for fishing. Others wanted to visit far-off coves and villages, swim, and sightsee. Some parties wanted to sail beyond the points of Banderas

Bay and into the open sea. Federico acquiesced to whatever they wanted, for he lacked a preference, no longer enjoyed the toil. His thoughts dwelled on the day Juan died.

"I don't fit in any longer," Federico told Teresa.

Later that winter four anglers from Arizona hired Federico. They fished for half a day in the southern part of the bay, then asked Federico to let them try their luck in the north. They would troll along the way. Federico set the throttle low, locked the wheel for the desired angle, and joined the fishermen at the rail, as he occasionally did.

"My wife praises the red snapper," Federico said in English.

The men had pulled in several fine specimens, but only Federico had a line in the water when he felt his bait being taken and jerked away. "A big one," he shouted.

The others gathered around. "Let him run awhile, Freddie," one said.

"Don't let him get away, Freddie," another contributed.

After the big fish swam far out it started back toward the boat. Federico hurriedly reeled in much of the line. The fish started out again. Federico braced himself and tugged.

One of the tourists took the wheel and steered the boat in a slow circle.

Federico and the fish dueled for an hour before he brought it alongside: a huge shark. He clubbed it in the head.

"That monster's going to be hard to get in the boat, Freddie."

"Yes. We tow him to beach near pier."

Twenty minutes later Federico's clients stepped off the boat into shallow water and towed the shark to the beach. Federico dropped anchor and joined them.

"What are you going to do, Freddie?"

"Take liver. Some people like it. Then I tow him to deep sea. Maybe he sinks."

The men watched. When Federico sliced open the shark he discovered large bones, red cloth that had been part of a swimsuit, and a medallion with chain.

Federico picked up the medallion. The front featured an angel with halo. He turned it over. Engraving said, "Juan Feliz."

When Federico handed Juan's medallion to Carmelita she fainted. He never told her about the bones and piece of swimsuit. But his clients that day talked to others, and the information, including the discovery of Juan's medallion, soon spread throughout the town.

He didn't leave home for several days. When he did, his walk to the pier became a chore of trying to reject unwanted congratulations for killing the shark that had carried off Juan Feliz.

At the end of each day when he walked toward home Federico received so many invitations to have a celebratory drink that he finally accepted one. This happened many times. In any cantina men crowded around, and some offered to buy him drinks, and as a courtesy he accepted one or two. Federico found the tequila to be as strong as the *raicilla* of San Miguel and to taste better. The men had lots of comments and questions.

"Do you think those were leg bones?"

"They say you also found his swimsuit in the shark's belly."

"Tell us about the medallion."

Federico touched his own medallion and took another sip. He had never been a center of attention. After a drink he liked the camaraderie, felt comfortable.

By the time the rainy season started, Federico habitually returned home late for supper. The children questioned their mother. One night after they had gone to bed, Teresa questioned Federico.

"You can't tell me you're still being forced into a cantina every day after work to repeat that horrible story about Juan and the shark."

"But I am," Federico said. "I can't avoid it. Sometimes."

"'Sometimes'? How about 'never'?"

Federico fidgeted. "I enjoy the companionship."

"Don't you enjoy our companionship?"

"Of course. The cantina is different. I fit in like I did fishing before Juan died."

"I would think everyone has heard that gruesome tale three times over by now."

Federico shrugged.

"Every night you come home later."

"I don't like to fish any longer. It's not the same."

"That situation won't change."

"So I reward myself with a little drink after work. I have so many friends now in the cantinas. And everyone says I'm a good guy."

"What I thought. And on Sundays we never go to the plaza anymore."

"That statue of Juan is too sad to see."

"We don't take the children for picnics up the river anymore."

"I'm tired after working all week."

"We don't go to the movies either."

"I would just go to sleep."

"Not if you'd quit drinking after work."

One night Teresa told him, "Federico, the children cry themselves to sleep every night."

"Why? What's wrong with them?"

"They cry for their father."

"But I . . ."

"And so do I."

Federico hurried to the nearest cantina.

The sun arrived robustly from behind the mountains. Its luster made his eyes ache to their roots. His head hurt from ear to ear. He turned onto his side, his back to the sun, and rested his head on his arm because the cobblestones of the gutter also hurt his head. Federico thought his stomach climbed into his chest and then into his throat. His head started swirling as though on a stick, and his stomach gyrated. Federico vomited.

He finished retching, closed his eyes, and took shallow breaths, not wanting to disturb his stomach again. When he opened his eyes he caught a movement nearby along the gutter. With effort he focused on his companion:

A buzzard enjoying the carcass of a large rat.

Two other buzzards stood near Federico. Their small black eyes watched him.

Federico shouted and waved his arm. The buzzards hopped along the street a short distance and stopped, looking back at him. When he shouted and waved again they hopped a few more times and ran until they could fly.

He quit watching them and slowly sat up, examined the trash in the gutter, studied the dead animal. *Would the buzzards have attacked me if I hadn't awakened?* He trembled, looked at his shaking hands, his dirty rumpled clothes. *They could have pecked my eyes out.*

He stood, vomited again, and walked unsteadily home. *I'll sell my boat. Have to.*

Far up the dirt path Federico Ponce stopped, setting down his bundle. Teresa and their children paused behind him, put down their bundles, stood quietly. Federico lifted his eyes to the familiar chicle and the ficus trees, the elephant ear and the palm and the banana. He couldn't see the corn-fields on the slopes of the next hills, but he felt at home knowing they were there. He studied his surroundings for a long time, thinking, wondering.

Federico turned, looking over the heads of Teresa and their children, saw a slice of the great bay. And he looked at Teresa. She nodded. Federico smiled and picked up his bundle. He squared his shoulders and continued up the trail. His family followed.

The statue of Juan Feliz in the central plaza has acquired the patina of age, and the town has grown. No one there remembers where Federico came from. Some recall him as "Freddie," though few know his correct name. They're not sure when he left nor where he went. But when people tell the story of Juan Feliz they usually mention the man they know so little about. They call him The Man Who Killed the Shark That Ate the Good Guy.

About This Time of Winter

"She's here again. Can we keep going?" When Mike nodded, Valerie squeezed his hand, and they continued walking until reaching stools at the other end of the Hotel Océano bar.

All stools permitted the same view, and the bartender never lingered but always took orders, brought the drinks, and returned to the register, where he didn't block anyone from enjoying the panorama: vast Banderas Bay just beyond the seawall, the water deep blue this time of afternoon, clouds preparing for a glorious sunset, pelicans gliding, searching, then briefly stalling beak-down before diving on their prey.

Sea gulls and terns assembled at the splashes the big hunters made and pilfered whatever the pelicans didn't gobble into that big suitcase under their beaks.

When the woman laughed, Valerie and Mike glanced her way, then back toward the bay.

"I think she's talking to herself," Valerie said.

"Not to the bartender?"

"I don't think so."

"Maybe she's been here too long." Mike sipped his tequila sour.

"Or not long enough. I could never be here too long."

"I'm with you."

Valerie elbowed him. "You'd better be." She kissed his cheek.

They sipped their tequila sours and watched the bay and the sea birds and the lowering sun, and the woman laughed again, softly, briefly.

"Like she's laughing to herself." Valerie slid off her stool.

"Where are you going?"

"She's lonesome, maybe upset. I'll just say hello and ask her to join us."

"I wouldn't."

"You're not a woman."

Valerie returned in a few moments. "'Thanks but no thanks.'"

"Told you."

"I'm glad I tried. She appreciated it."

"What's she laughing about?"

"We didn't get chummy."

The tables and chairs filled, and the bar stools had been taken except the one they saved for George Pease. The sun would be touching the far horizon within minutes when he joined them.

"We were afraid you'd be late." Mike patted the adjacent stool.

"Got wrapped up in some correspondence." George sat. "But I kept one eye on the west. What did you kiddies do today?" George motioned for the bartender.

"Swam. Sunned. Sat under a *palapa* at Los Muertos and read, Mickey Spillane for me, Faulkner for Valerie. She's smarter than me."

"I've noticed."

The bartender took George's order and left just as the woman at the other end of the bar laughed, more of an explosion this time and imposing itself over the commotion in the cantina.

Valerie looked at Mike, who shook his head and smiled.

They watched the bay and the sea birds, and Valerie silently estimated the time remaining before the sun turned the clouds into shades of red, pink, and yellow, and she wondered if a green flash would also entertain them. They told George of their college studies and how they needed this hiatus between semesters. George, an engineer in the US Maritime Service, sketched his approaching assignment.

"I needed a good vacation," George said. "And I wanted to see you two."

Valerie leaned in to look her way when the woman laughed again. "Someone's sitting next to her, but he's speaking to the woman on his left."

"Who are you talking about?" George asked.

"The lady at the other end. She's upset about something, laughing but unhappy."

George looked toward the woman. "Oh. Mrs. Gray. She must have been in the ladies' when I came in. Yes. She's upset all right, has been for a long time."

The bartender brought George a jigger of white Sauza on ice.

"She seems so sad," Valerie said.

George sipped, set down his glass. "I remember now. You and Mike just missed her last year. But she did the same thing. Eerie, that laughter, when you don't know. It's an interesting story. And I had a front row seat."

Valerie looked past Mike to see George more clearly. *Is George studying the bay? Anticipating the sunset? Organizing his thoughts?* "Tell us, George."

"Mrs. Gray." George nodded, continued to watch the water. "Mrs. Jason Gray, Dorothy, early fifties. Nice lady. Good sense of humor. Widow of a wealthy California aerospace manufacturer, components, subcontractor a few years older, big, gregarious.

"They'd fly down here every winter and stay a month, no kids, always rented the same house in Gringo Gulch with a matchless view. Just about everyone in Puerto Vallarta seemed to know them. They'd swim and hike and fish. Sometimes at the airport Mrs. Gray would sit at the bar and sip coffee while Gray monkeyed with their red-and-white Cessna, a four-seater."

Mike said, "Sounds like 'inseparable' would fit them."

"Yep. I wish I'd had a marriage like that."

"Did they give parties? Is that how you knew them?"

"In a small resort town like this, just walking around you acquire a nodding acquaintance with folks. When they stay a while, the way the Grays did, and as I do, you sometimes gravitate toward one another. They'd often come in here to watch a sunset. We caught a few green flashes together. They were low key. I liked that."

Again, Dorothy Gray's laughter reached them.

"The poor woman," Valerie said. "She could be so pretty if she tried."

"She's hardly been sober enough lately to care. The neighbors say she starts her serious drinking after climbing the hill to her house."

"She must have friends. Won't anyone help her?"

"Says she doesn't need any help. When she gets sick enough I suppose they'll be able to get her to the hospital." He sipped his drink. "About three years ago they met a mechanical engineer from Chicago, a guy named Olson and around Jason Gray's age and also a pilot. They hit it off. Gray had to go to Guadalajara to meet a couple of associates on their way to Mexico City. He invited Olson to accompany him.

"I witnessed some of what I'm saying. Other stuff I heard later. Anyway, it's a ninety-minute flight to Guadalajara, and they took off at dawn. Gray's associates picked them up at the airport in a rental car, and they spent several hours in the restaurant and bar at the Hotel Fénix, where Gray's friends lodged."

In the early afternoon, George said, Gray's associates had to leave for Mexico City, and they all went together to the Guadalajara airport, where Gray and Olson later would also take off, in their case to return to Puerto Vallarta.

"It was about this time of winter. You know how quick it gets dark here when the sun goes down. And the airport doesn't have lights. You just don't fly in here after dark. But I'd been sitting right here remembering the great sunset when I heard the engine. There must have barely been light enough to get the plane past the mountain.

"Maybe Gray had misjudged the remaining daylight. Lights were on, so he could find the town easy enough, and I learned later some airport employees drove cars onto the edge of the landing strip and turned on the headlights. Maybe the little illumination he saw at the airport didn't satisfy him, however, so he passed on it."

The plane's lights and engine noise broadcast the aircraft's whereabouts.

"He flew low over the water right here in front of us." George motioned toward the bay. "Full dark closed in on the plane by the second. We had a new moon and a high tide, little natural light and no hard-packed sand to land on. I wanted a better look. I hurried out of here to a small spot a little farther south where the beach slopes up a lot, and high tide doesn't reach it. Others had already got there, among them Dorothy Gray.

"The plane circled over the bay and came in low in front of us over shallow water. To our left he nearly hit the boulders on that little promontory called El Púlpito. Dorothy and a lot of others cried out, but he pulled up and headed back out over the bay. I heard Dorothy tell the woman near her that Gray buzzed the town so she would know he'd returned, saying good-bye."

"Sad," Valerie said.

Mrs. Gray's activities of mourning again reached them.

She stepped off the bar stool, laughed again, took a deep breath. She squared her shoulders, arched her back, manufactured a crooked smile for the bartender, and left.

"He banked the plane and flew parallel to shore again, not even fifty yards out and much slower. We could see him easy, and lights from hotels and other businesses reflected off the bay for quite a distance. The wheels nearly touched the water. Some of us figured Gray planned to pancake onto the bay. I don't know what else he could have done, and if the plane didn't break up badly he and Olson might not get hurt and would have a chance to get out before it sank.

"With the nose up he cut the engine. The Cessna glided some, then smacked hard onto the water, skidded a bit, and began to submerge. I glanced at Dorothy standing nearby with a flashlight. Its beam struck the sand in front of her. She gasped."

George paused. "Let's watch this a minute."

The sun seemed to touch the water and begin to sink. They watched without speaking, as did most of the patrons. Soon it flattened out, spreading yellow and orange to each side and into the sky. When the sun blinked and disappeared, the clouds became pink and red with tints of yellow.

"No green flash," Mike said, "but another beauty."

"Now finish, George."

"Several small boats with motors had been beached on that same high slope, so some of us dragged two into the water. The owners had been watching with us, and we got both motors started. When we reached the spot where the plane struck the water some of the men shined flashlights around. We found a piece of cowling, what looked like some of the horizontal stabilizer, and small pieces of metal we couldn't identify."

"Nothing else?" Mike said.

George shook his head. "We circled the spot and shined flashlights around in case Gray or Olson clung to a piece of wreckage. The bay's deep. No one mentioned diving in. Then we spotted a box tied by ribbon, like something from a store. We took it to shore and learned it contained a blue cocktail dress. For Gray's wife or Olson's? Mrs. Gray glanced at it and shook her head ambiguously. Her neighbors started walking her home.

"Someone notified the captain of the port, and he requested divers from the Mexican Coast Guard to examine the wreckage for bodies. The divers were said to be on the way, but this is Mexico. The next day a fisherman found a body in the water and brought it in. Sharks had done a job on it, the face obliterated, big chunks chewed off both legs.

"This place doesn't have a morgue, so the body waited at the hospital. Because the police think I know everyone they asked me to identify the corpse, and I took a look. Gray and Olson were about the same size, and because the face had been ruined they got no help from me. They sent for Dorothy Gray."

"Uh-oh," Valerie said. "I can imagine what's coming."

"Maybe not," George told her. "Being nosy I stuck around. Nobody cared. The doctor suggested she not look at the face but try to identify the body by jewelry, scars or birthmarks, clothing. Mrs. Gray, fighting back tears, nodded and stepped close. The doctor pulled off the sheet except over the face. Mrs. Gray examined the body, shook her head, and paused. All of a sudden she cried out and started laughing, couldn't stop. Next she started crying, couldn't stop crying either. Finally she got hold of herself.

"'It must be Olson,' she said. 'Thank God it's not my husband.'"

Her tears and laughter had been in relief. The shirt, torn and bloody, could still be recognized as chartreuse. Her husband never wore that color because she despised it. Olson, however, wore a chartreuse shirt to Guadalajara.

"So Mr. Gray's body," Valerie said, "remained in the plane?"

"It looked like it. But when the divers got there they found the wreckage empty. And his body never showed up anywhere. She knew she'd lost him but could pretend he rested peacefully somewhere, undamaged, maybe waiting for her on the other side."

"What happened to her?" Mike asked.

"Mrs. Gray went home to California. But she returned before spring, came back to stay. Her friends thought she'd recuperate better in a different atmosphere. But she and Gray had been everywhere that interested her. If he were going to be with her mentally, the way she wanted, it might as well be in the place that had become paradise for them."

"Surely," Valerie said, "she hasn't been drinking so heavily for three years."

"No. She seemed normal. She socialized. Oh, once in a while accompanied by a gin and tonic she'd walk down to the water's edge and stand there looking out toward the crash area. She must have suffered lots of weak moments. But last year, shortly after you two left, Mrs. Gray received a letter that hit her like a rocket. That's what started her marathon binge. The letter, addressed to her and Gray, came from Olson."

The man presumed to have perished with Jason Gray wrote that he had elected to go to Mexico City with Gray's associates. Gray, eager to rejoin his wife, would hurry off to Puerto Vallarta. Olson would telegraph him a few days later to return for him.

"In Mexico City the men checked in at the Hotel del Prado, admired Diego Rivera's mural about Alameda Park, and took a taxi to Garibaldi Plaza for a night of mariachi music, Mexican food, and general revelry. Olson wrote that he had a difficult time getting out of the Bar Tenampa. He drank too much, made a fool of himself, tussled with the cops trying to make him leave, and sat for three days in jail.

"After being released he spent three more days in his hotel

room with the *turistas* while fretting about his business, then hurried home. Olson saw no need to contact Gray, whom he hardly knew and who he assumed had forgotten him. In Chicago authorities had been notified of Olson's death, so he stunned his family when he showed up in a sarape and a big sombrero with conchos. Imagine their shock and joy. But the incorrect report caused entanglements in his business, and he had his hands full straightening them out."

Despite the brief acquaintanceship, George said, Olson wrote that he realized he liked the other fellow and his wife, one of those serendipitous Mexican connections that turn out to last a long time. He wanted to visit them in Mexico if they could forgive him for his callous French leave and not keeping in touch. Olson added an anecdote.

"He remembered kidding Gray about being so eager to see his wife after a separation of only a few hours that he owed her a treat. Gray purchased a cocktail dress for her. Then he decided to add a little devilment before he'd let her see the dress, and so he bought himself a chartreuse shirt.

"Olson recalled that Gray said something like, 'My wife has a great sense of humor, and sometimes I tease her. She can't stand chartreuse so I'll be wearing it when she meets me at the airport. She'll squawk when she first sees me, but later she'll have a terrific laugh.'"

Antonia

◇◇◇◇◇◇◇◇◇◇◇◇◇

George Pease had often noticed her through the windows of the little restaurant or waiting on customers at the outside tables near the path he walked to reach the center of town or return to the Hotel Delicias. He had seen her at the alfresco market purchasing fruit and vegetables. And once he passed near when she sat in the central plaza eating a mango, skin and all, while leaning to the side and holding it so it wouldn't drip on her dress.

She appealed to him. He wanted to ask her out.

And several times he had listed the obstacles to his doing so. *My Spanish is poorer than the ragpickers at the dump . . . Maybe she'd feel out of place with a gringo . . . Maybe I'd feel out of place with her . . . She's too young to be interested in a forty-year-old bald-headed sailor like me. Perhaps I shouldn't even try because I have to leave in a few weeks to catch my ship. But so what? And, hell, she might even be married or have a boyfriend. So why am I fretting?*

So again he merely glanced toward her workplace, El Gran Café Camino Real, glimpsed her serving a shirtless young barefoot Mexican. *Whoever named that place had a sense of humor. The only thing grand about it is the waitress. And if this trail is the royal highway the Hotel Delicias is the Beverly Hilton.*

George thought she looked more attractive than usual, prettier, spunky, saucy, ponytail bouncing as she started back inside. He wished she had looked up so he could wave or nod. *But she's probably not thinking about me the way I am about her. She's sure pretty, though.*

While he walked through town, past the plaza, and on to the Hotel Océano he continued thinking about her. As he sat in the Océano dining room after his meal and sipped a Corona while absorbing the beauty of the sunset he imagined her face, her movements. And in the increasing dark during his return trip to his hotel George developed a plan that would either open his gate of hesitation and allow him to ask her out—or he would learn that the gate would remain locked no matter how furiously he shook it.

George had dined in San Francisco at Il Fiore di Italia, in New Orleans at Antoine's, in New York at Elaine's, in Paris at Deux Magots. In Singapore he had relaxed on the veranda of the Raffles Hotel while enjoying a gin and tonic, and in Taormina he sat under an umbrella on the beach while absorbing the beauty of the bay. Each storied place filled him with excitement, as had friendships with certain women. But he could not recall the nervousness he now experienced when he turned off the dirt road, stepped along the sandy path lined by Rain of Gold shrubs—yellow spots freckling their lush verdant leaves—and approached the small Mexican eatery, simple and rustic, that bravely called itself El Gran Café Camino Real. His palms perspired.

Wearing shorts, Hawaiian shirt, and huaraches, George took an outside table, the only customer, though at midafternoon he had often seen the place crowded, apparently with laborers. He placed his wide-brimmed straw hat on the table, for the sun had barely debuted and his hairless pate wouldn't blister, and sat so he could watch passersby, the bay, the birds of the sea, and the occasional sailboat or fishing vessel.

He could also keep an eye on the interior of the restaurant. That is, he could watch the waitress moving around inside. *I don't expect much in the way of food. But they shouldn't be able to mess up breakfast. And I'll enjoy a close look at her and be able to exchange a couple of words. Maybe she knows a little English. While I wait I'll keep busy shooing away the flies. Shouldn't be any cockroaches this far from the kitchen.*

She wore a green-and-white dress and red apron he'd previously seen on her. And when she waited on him George enjoyed his first close look: in her mid-twenties, inquisitive brown eyes complementing smooth coppery skin, red ribbon mastering her ponytail. And her smile exploded when she spoke, bloomed huge and bright like the sun that had just risen from behind the Sierra Madre Occidental.

"It's about time," she said.

George looked up in pleasure and confusion. *Speaks English. Good.* "Time for what?"

"That you finally stopped here for a meal. You pass by all the time."

"You noticed." He waved away a fly.

"Of course."

He felt flattered and awkward, sought an excuse, didn't want to mention his concern about flies and cockroaches. "It's just that I've had the habit of walking into town for meals."

"Yes. For a long time." Her smile bloomed again.

George laughed. "I guess I could have at least examined your menu."

"No menu. Breakfast and lunch only. But Aunt can cook anything. Just not fancy."

"I'm not fancy either."

"Good. I am Antonia Carrasco. What would you like?"

I think I'd like an Antonia Carrasco. "My name is—I'm George Pease. How about coffee first, black, American style? Then huevos rancheros with chorizo and corn tortillas."

"Aunt can do that." She scared a fly off the table. "'Peace' in Spanish is '*paz*.'"

"Actually it's spelled a little different."

"No matter. Aunt and I call you Jorge Paz. You drive big boats on the Seven Seas and you come to Mexico for long periods and always stay at the Delicias even though you could afford a nice hotel. You're not married, and sometimes you drink too much."

George smiled. "How do you know all that?"

"Aunt sleeps with Don Paco."

"And who is this splendidly informed Don Paco?"

"He owns the Delicias, lives downstairs on this end. You talk with him a little."

"Very little, though he knows some English. Mr. Alcaide. I've learned that he fought in the Spanish Civil War. He never mentioned your aunt."

Antonia nodded. "He showed Aunt some old newspaper clippings from Córdoba, his home. He fought so hard they called him The Army of the East." She turned to leave, stopped, and told him, "Look out for flies."

George laughed, enjoyed the swirl of her departure, studied his surroundings: the whitewashed wooden restaurant, the edge of corrugated tin protruding under the roof of palm fronds, the living quarters above one end of the structure. Through large windows he counted four tables inside, looked at the chipped red paint of the square wooden table near him and of the one he occupied. He liked the papayas and banana trees around the exterior and the purple bougainvillea climbing to the roof in the rear, admired the Castilian rose near the front door.

And he caught Antonia smiling at him from the entry.

George liked the way she had identified herself: not "My name is" but "I am," and with her last name too. *Pride. Confidence.* So he watched out for the flies, for Antonia too, and when he finished had to be careful to leave a small tip only, Mexican style in a restaurant like that.

He also risked the flies on the following mornings for what he thought of as breakfast with Antonia. Her smile and friendliness never changed, and she always revisited his table to see if he wanted anything else, mainly stayed occupied inside with other customers and in the kitchen. George guessed she also made busywork. *Maybe she pretends to have things to do because the aunt is a tyrant, might think Antonia's flirting with me. That would be nice.*

And each morning George determined that would be the time he asked her to dinner. But even after his third consecutive breakfast, including a second cup of coffee at the end of each, he vacillated. *Why has this kid got me buffaloed? And she's not even trying. Hell, she's old enough to go out with me. Mexican women like older men. Maybe tomorrow will be a better time to ask.*

With the tab George placed money, including a tip larger than usual. He stood, put on his hat, would have waved good-bye to Antonia except he couldn't locate her through the windows. So he walked the Rain of Gold path, and at the dirt road turned toward the Hotel Delicias. *Damn it.* Then: *Oh, hell.* He turned back toward El Gran Café Camino Real, this time could see her, and he strode to the table he had occupied.

With a smile and a curious look Antonia met him there.

George removed his hat. "Will you go to dinner with me tonight?"

Antonia laughed lightly. *"*Of course.*"*

George decided to take Antonia to Flor de Vallarta, a bayside eatery a short walk toward the town. *This girl would look good in the finest restaurant at the best hotel, but I don't think either of us would be comfortable.* "It's all banana trees and palms. Rustic. Small. The food can't be beat, and few tourists have discovered it."

"Which is why you like it."

"Probably. The view's great too. And it's well priced."

"That doesn't matter to you. Don Paco told Aunt you have a mountain of money."

"I see." George hadn't noticed her accent much in brief exchanges. But now he heard it clearly. He liked her speech, her tone, the slight accent, her occasional literal interpretation from Spanish.

When the unpaved road bent toward the automobile bridge over the Río Cuale they turned onto the path to the rickety footbridge, crossed that narrow contraption Indian file, and soon stood at the restaurant entry. George admired the reboant waves, identical siblings to those in front of the hotel where he lodged, and he liked the breeze, the smell of the sea. George also enjoyed the way the full moon turned much of the water into a silvery platter—until realizing she watched him instead of the view. "Let's go inside, Antonia Carrasco."

The waiter took them to a corner window table decorated by a red rose in a bud vase and by a short fat candle, red and well used, supplementing light from a Tiffany-style swag lamp. Potted palms and banana trees filled spaces along the walls and at the edges of a small wooden dance floor. Two other couples occupied corner tables.

"This is nice, Jorge Paz. I've only seen it from the outside when I walk into town."

George wondered why no one had ever brought her there, found himself feeling pleased that none had. *Maybe she's new in town. Maybe her friends think it's expensive. And why do I think she has only low-budget friends? I believe I'll quit thinking.* "Want a drink?"

"A beer would fall good to me."

George smiled at what he accepted as another literal interpretation, realized he didn't feel awkward around her. He ordered each a Sol, and they examined menus. "I can vouch for the carne asada."

"'Vouch'?"

"It's like to approve or guarantee."

"OK. Will it be as good as Aunt's?"

"I've never tasted your aunt's steaks. But I can guarantee it will arrive without flies."

Antonia smiled. "As long as it arrives with beans and rice, a little guacamole."

George ordered the carne asada dinner for each, and the waiter left. "I need to clarify something your aunt heard from her observant informant Don Paco, or maybe she misunderstood. Anyway, I don't drive ships. Another fellow, the boss, the captain, he does that. We carry cargo. What I do is keep the engines in good shape so the boss can do his job."

"OK, but if you didn't do that, the *capitán* couldn't drive."

"No. So he'd get a different engineer." He sipped his beer. "Now your turn."

"My 'turn'?"

"You know more than enough about me. I want to hear about you." *How is it that you are so feminine, almost dainty, yet with an underlying toughness, a steely strength?*

Antonia sipped her beer, looked at the moonlit bay, faced George. "I tell you some. Sorry if you no like me."

"Tell me some. I already like you." *How could I not? Sleeveless décolleté blue dress hugging a trim frame, hair in a long smooth ponytail held by a yellow ribbon, not one piece of jewelry marring her satiny skin, just a dab of lipstick, and that sunburst of a smile.*

"I'm here three months to live with my aunt and work with her. I have, I'm twenty-four. I have a daughter seven. She lives with my older sister and her husband in

Guadalajara, *mi patria chica*. I miss her all the minutes."
Antonia addressed the bay. "My daughter's name is Dulce.
She is *muy inteligente* and she likes school. Dulce is going
to be a doctor, I think, or a big movie star like Dolores del
Río at least. I love her too much." She again faced George,
smiled feebly, sipped her beer.

He nodded, and the waiter brought their meals. *So many
more questions now. But I'd better save them for next time, if
there is one.* "You know a lot of English and use it well."

"Mexico is not always . . . What is the word? Behind?"

"Backward."

"*Sí.* They teach a little English in the first six grades, and
you can learn a lot if you try. I tried and I learned. And I
have worked in places with tourists, mostly Americans and
English. Do I sound American or English?"

"Will you settle for a little of each?"

She tilted her head and smiled. "*Bien.*"

When they finished eating, George walked to a stand-
up jukebox of a kind he had seldom seen in recent years. It
accepted US coins and had been stacked with tunes American as well as Mexican, in English and Spanish. He inserted
a quarter and punched five numbers.

You Belong to My Heart, which George saw listed in both
languages, began playing before he turned toward their table.
When he reached it Antonia stood, took his hand, and led
him to the dance floor. Another couple joined them there.

"I'm not real good at this," George said.

"Neither am I."

He held her, and they moved slowly, and George avoided
stepping on her. "I thought you weren't good at this."

Antonia squeezed his hand and moved closer. "How
many songs did you play?"

He told her.

"Let's dance to all of them."

They danced to all of them, and Antonia asked him for

a quarter. She played five more, each a standard, old like the jukebox. George recognized *Amor* and *Bésame Mucho,* couldn't recall the names of the next two, but knew the fifth, *Begin the Beguine.* He felt they moved closer together with each step of that bewitching tune.

When *Begin the Beguine* ended she didn't release his hand.

He liked that. "Should I spend some more quarters?"

"It would please me, Jorge Paz. But I have to get up so early."

George left a generous tip. They stepped into the night, and Antonia took his hand while they walked along the trail parallel to shore. Moonlight on the water and in the sky, as well as expiring waves whispering musically, accompanied them.

Neither spoke much, though George had questions with each step. He wondered if Antonia also did. So they strolled that way, holding hands, talking little. They maneuvered the footbridge once more, soon could see El Gran Café Camino Real. At the connecting path lined by the Rain of Gold, George stopped, Antonia beside him.

George considered what to say, what to do. He wanted to take her out again. *Will she go out again if I ask? Is the experiment with the loafing gringo over? She had enjoyed the dancing, relished her meal, said her aunt could create none better.* Her hand still warm in his had not loosened.

George glanced over her head at the bay, the moonlight, looked down at her, saw her smile in the diaphanous dark. "Thanks for the great evening, Antonia Carrasco."

"It's not over is it?" She tiptoed and lightly kissed him, then tugged his hand and motioned with her head toward the Hotel Delicias.

In the predawn light, air redolent with the smell of the sea, waves smacking the nearby shore, the sheet kicked beyond their feet, Antonia explained her scars to George.

"This one." She touched her left breast. "I talked in a cantina with friends, our regular place, not a cave of *vicios*. And I got in a fight with another girl. She stabbed me. It really hurt."

"I would think so. What happened next?"

"I took the knife away from her and stuck it in her belly."

"I see." *Is this the girl who dined so happily with me last night? Who danced so warmly? Who made love so tenderly?* "And then what?"

"The police took us to hospital, then to jail. I am home for breakfast." Antonia laughed. "My father knew the chief."

George, propped on an elbow, lay beside her, studied her, Antonia on her back, ponytail undone, long black hair spread over the pillow. *Probably raised poor in some Guadalajara barrio, though trouble is everywhere. Or maybe there's family money but she's been exiled.*

"This one." Antonia touched her jawbone near an inchlong horizontal scar, narrow, like a slice, whitened by time. "My boyfriend and I were arguing, and he hit me here."

"I think I'd like to talk to that young man." *What in hell am I thinking?* "Just arguing?"

"I was right and he didn't know what else to say. Mexicans are that way."

"I hope you quit seeing him."

"No. He is Dulce's father. But I didn't like him much anymore. And my father told him he'd better not hurt me again or he would be disappeared. Finally I don't see him. But he visits Dulce, and that's good." She touched a horizontal line on her lower abdomen. "For Dulce."

"A cesarean."

"That's the word. Now you."

"Are you finished already?"

Antonia laughed, placed her hand on George's hip.

"All right. But I'm relatively undamaged. Just an appendectomy when I was a kid."

"Lucky. But why don't you have any hair on your coco?" She rubbed his head.

"I have some. But it looks funny, so I shave it."

"I like it. Did you have a sickness? You're not old."

"No, just the accident of how the family genes got together. My father's bald."

For the remainder of George's stay they spent every night in his hotel room. Antonia always left when she heard Don Paco's rooster crow from its pen near the other end of the hotel, for she had to help her aunt with breakfast customers.

"Besides," Antonia told George, "we have hot water, not just a cold shower like at this wobbly old Hotel Delicias."

George ate all his breakfasts at her workplace, leaving an increasingly larger tip each time until Antonia asked him not to. They dined out nightly, sampling every Mexican eatery in the town, including several returns to the Flor de Vallarta. He often took his camera and photographed her. But Antonia would never agree to dine at the Hotel Océano.

"The Océano is too *grande* for me."

"It is not. You have to see the sunset from there."

"No."

"Why not?"

"Because."

Late one afternoon for a few pesos George purchased two freshly caught red snappers from a fisherman who cleaned them, skewered them on green sticks, and cooked them over a fire on the beach. The breeze delivered a salty fragrance from the bay to meld with the provocative aroma of the sizzling fish. The fisherman provided salt and sliced limes. George brought the beer and tortillas. They watched the sunset while eating with their fingers.

"Thank you, Jorge Paz. This is my best evening ever."

That night in George's room Antonia showed him several black-and-white photos of her daughter. "Here we're at the circus. That one's outside the Basílica de Guadalajara. Here she is in a long skirt with lots of colors like the big singer Lola Beltrán. Here's one in front of Dulce's school. My sister took it, the one Dulce lives with. That's me beside my daughter."

"I can tell. She's pretty like you."

"I wanted one of me at her school because I didn't go to school much."

George watched her study the photo, small like the others, but this one showing signs of extensive handling. *She needs a better camera. And no doubt many other things.* "Since you've been here have you gone back to see her?"

Antonia shook her head. "Aunt needs me right now. Then I go. I miss Dulce too much."

"Someday will you live in Guadalajara again, have Dulce with you?"

She shrugged. "I hope so."

Antonia asked George to photograph her—before she dressed.

He obliged.

George wore long pants, dress shirt, and shoes for the first time in two months. He hung his camera around his neck, left his duffle bag and satchel packed and on the bed with his straw hat and light coat, and walked the few steps to the restaurant.

At an outside table when Antonia waited on him he thought she seemed distant despite having only recently left his bed. He still felt her kisses. *But that's the trouble. We've said our good-byes, and who knows when we'll meet again, or if. I think she feels the same, although she wouldn't say much, not with words. I'll do my part, like I told her. But it could be six months before I can come back. And where will this vagabond be by then? Could I find her in Guadalajara? Would she want me to? And which of us is the vagabond?*

George shooed away a fly, thought *South of the Border* while humming *El Paso* and mentally reprising one line: "I fell in love with a Mexican girl." He requested American-style coffee, chorizo, tortillas, and eggs scrambled with tomato sauce, goat cheese sprinkled on top.

Antonia returned inside. She had secured her ponytail with a green ribbon,

George didn't try to talk with her until she brought his check. "I have a small gift for you." He stood.

"Not necessary." Antonia had pinned a red rose to her bodice.

He handed her his camera. "It has a new roll of film."

"No, Jorge Paz. That's expensive. I can tell."

"Please accept it. I'm going to get a newer one. And I have something for Dulce."

"You shouldn't."

"I walked into town yesterday to get it. She deserves it. I feel like I know her well."

"All right. Thank you."

"I'm not good at buying things for girls or women."

She smiled. "*Bien.*"

George removed an envelope from his shirt pocket and slipped it into the pocket on Antonia's apron.

"Are you sure it's for Dulce?" Antonia said.

"As certain as the sea is deep. Call it a scholarship."

"I have something for you." She unpinned the rose from her bodice and attached it to George's shirt pocket. "I'm not good at buying gifts for men." Her smile became the sunburst she often greeted him with.

"Nothing could be better, Antonia Carrasco."

"Good sailing, Jorge Paz."

From the backseat of the taxi to the airport George tried to see Antonia once more, couldn't locate her, assumed she had duties in the restaurant kitchen.

Two thousand dollars in pesos. That should help her and Dulce a lot until I come here again. I hope she'll be here.

The taxi rolled across the bridge over the Río Cuale.

George hummed the lyrics about falling in love with a Mexican girl.

THE ARMY OF THE EAST

"It's exasperating and it's my own damn fault. All the time I've spent here over the years I should have learned Spanish long ago." He leaned against the kitchen sink at El Gran Café Camino Real, George sipping coffee, Agripina chopping vegetables for a stew whose ingredients would feature bites of grilled pork.

"You are not alone with that problem, Jorge Paz. Don't flail yourself like some penitent during Holy Week."

"But I like history. Sometimes on the ship I read more than I work. I've always been interested in the Spanish Civil War because my favorite uncle fought in it with one of the international brigades. Thing is I was too young to enjoy his stories. Something about Barcelona and eastern Spain is all I remember. Now I wish I'd paid attention."

George sipped his coffee, watched her slide chopped vegetables into the stew pot, and continued. "Don Paco tries to help. He fought in it. You know that. Once in a while I hear 'Communist' or 'Franco' or 'Río Ebro.' But I just . . . and his accent . . ."

"Andalucía. He couldn't lose it any more than he could forget his mother's smile." Her voice evoked Antonia's, and George could see Antonia in her aunt's face, in the youthful Agripina's gestures, her figure.

Antonia had told him Agripina and her husband left

Guadalajara to establish the restaurant in the idyllic community at the rim of Banderas Bay—and how the husband ran off with a wealthy American tourist.

"A man-thief half his age," Agripina had said.

Antonia also said her aunt and Don Paco were lovers.

However, despite George's time spent around this restaurant because of Antonia Carrasco, he barely knew Agripina, could hardly ask a favor. Antonia would return in three weeks from visiting her daughter in Guadalajara and could ask her aunt to interpret for George. *But I can't wait. I might get a telegram ordering me back to the ship. She speaks English as well as Antonia does. She could do it. But . . .* And George Pease, whom Antonia and Agripina called Jorge Paz, liked to understand a subject fully once he took it up.

The earlier life of Don Paco, a quiet man always a gentleman, had probed at George's mind ever since he learned tidbits of Paco's youth. Now George felt the urge to know right away or the hotel owner's story could be lost to him. *If I don't return, or if something happens to him, his experiences will be as lost to me as my uncle's, become as inaccessible as an anchor on a broken chain settling in the mud of Davy Jones's locker. But if I get Don Paco's story I'll feel as though I finally have my uncle's. And I'll stop castigating myself for not listening when I had the chance.*

He fidgeted, finished his coffee, looked over his shoulder toward customers at the inside tables, wished again he knew Agripina well enough to ask a favor. "Guess I'll walk the beach. I suppose I—"

"Meet me in Paco's office just after sunset," Agripina said. "He likes you. He will tell you about his time in the Civil War of Spain. And I will interpret for you, Jorge Paz."

Still excited about the previous evening's meeting with Agripina and Don Paco, George took his usual outside table at El Gran Café Camino Real. The waitress had brought coffee and returned inside when the younger man, Stanley Simpson, walking on the dirt road, turned off at the path lined by Rain of Gold and sat at George's table just as George started to invite him to do so.

"I started into town for breakfast," Stanley said, "but when I saw you here I assumed the place wouldn't poison me."

"Ðon't bet on it," George Pease told him. "But the breakfasts have been safe so far."

"What's the attraction, anyway? Proximity to the hotel? Cheap?"

"The tranquility. The early rush of laborers is over when I get here. I don't eat lunch, and I go into town for dinner. They don't serve dinner anyway. *Of course Antonia is the main attraction. But I wouldn't tell him that any more than I'd let him marry my sister.*

"Yesterday when we met you told me you'd been here awhile. So what's there to do?"

Before George could answer, the waitress, fiftyish and plump, slow but smiling, substituting for Antonia, brought his plate of chorizo, toast, grape jelly, and eggs scrambled in a sauce of tomatoes, onions, and goat cheese. She looked at Stanley.

"I'll have the same," he said. "And first thing an American coffee. Make sure it's hot."

She raised an eyebrow, looked at George.

He invoked one of the terms Antonia had taught him, "*Lo mismo, Celia,*" and he pointed at his own plate.

"*Gracias, Don Jorge Paz.*" Celia returned inside.

"What'd she say? I understood *gracias.*"

"Just some Mexican wordplay with my name."

"I brought a little dictionary. I'd better start carrying it."

Good thinking, Stanley. "You'll get by in some places without it. There's more tourism every time I'm here. You asked what's to do. How about loafing, reading, swimming, fishing, walking the beach north and south, hiking up the mountain?" *Studying your dictionary.*

"That can't be all. How about disco clubs?"

"There's a couple of brothels up the slope east of town. They usually play the radio."

He waved away George's comment. "Where's the best place to meet women?"

"I just told you."

"I don't mean pros. What about you? How do you pass the time? I saw every corner of this place yesterday afternoon, didn't realize Puerto Vallarta could be so small and quiet."

If you wanted Acapulco you should have gone to Acapulco. "I always have a good book. I talk to certain people—in English. I walk the beaches, swim a little. And I never miss a sunset."

"And that's all?"

"It's enough for me. Oh, some of the tourists get drunk twice a day."

Celia brought Stanley's breakfast and coffee, replenished George's coffee. He thanked her.

"Things might get lively soon," George said. "There's talk a bunch of Hollywood types, actors and film crew, the works, are coming to town to make a movie."

"No kidding? Hey, they'll probably have at least a small role for a guy like me."

George sipped his coffee, studied the birds of the sea, and watched the newcomer eat while shooing flies from his plate.

In a few minutes a passerby on the road caught George's attention. They exchanged waves, and the man continued walking. He wore long-sleeved white dress shirt, black slacks, shiny black shoes, and black flat-brimmed hat with a flat crown, *el sombrero cordobés.*

Stanley Simpson chased off another fly. "I'm never eating here again. Who's the duded-up old Mexican?"

"He's a Spaniard. Don Paco."

"Who is?"

"The man you paid your rent to yesterday when you checked in at the Delicias. He owns the place."

"Didn't recognize him. Looks different."

"You caught him in shorts and huaraches. Now he's wearing his business attire. Probably going to the bank or to see the mayor."

"Skinny little guy."

"Just trim. And you're tall, so he might seem little. Good man. Lots of class."

"Looks like he lives a boring life, probably always has."

If you only knew. And I won't enlighten you, the way you asked about five-star service at that dumpy little hotel, asked loudly because he didn't understand you. But there was a time . . .

When the Spanish Civil War started in 1936 Francisco Alcaide Rambla, now known in various areas of Mexico as Don Paco, belonged to a large family with investments in agriculture throughout the province of Córdoba. He immediately enlisted in the army of the Republic, received a commission and orders to report to Barcelona to help defend eastern Spain.

"I didn't want to go east," he had told Agripina and George that night. "I preferred to stay in Córdoba, defend my home province. But you don't always get what you want in the army."

They sat in his office on the ground floor at the east end of the building, an abandoned United Fruit Co. barracks Don Paco purchased the day he reached the town and which he renovated and christened the Hotel Delicias. One desk photo showed people whose attire and weathered faces told George they were men and women of the soil. Another had captured younger men and a woman who could be their mother. A framed photograph of the Roman Bridge over the Río Guadalquivir in Córdoba hung on one wall, and an unframed magazine photo of a mournful bullfighter, elegant, slim, had been pinned to another wall.

Paco, in short pants, huaraches, and a blue short-sleeved shirt, and smoking one of the American cigarettes George had brought him, set out three jiggers and filled them with Kahlúa.

George had never seen Agripina without her kitchen scarf around her head. Now he noticed how pretty she looked.

Pausing frequently so Agripina could interpret, Don Paco blamed the conflict on fascists and other right-wing interests claiming Spain teetered on turning Communist even though only three Communists sat in the Spanish *cortes*. Russia, Paco said, aided the Republican forces but did not control them.

He recounted the terror residents felt especially from the savage Moors of Spanish Morocco fighting for Gen. Francisco Franco's insurgent army.

Paco spoke of soldiers dead and dying on both sides, of attacks by German and Italian fighter planes and bombers. He told of the bombings endured and terrors suffered by civilians in Barcelona and other cities along the Mediterranean shore.

"Franco captured Mallorca right away," he said. "The planes came from there. Italians."

He told of trench warfare and artillery bombardments and described outrages, including murders of innocents, among them the execution of a famous poet and playwright, perhaps because of his poem denigrating the Spanish Civil Guard. Paco mentioned food shortages.

"All in books," Paco said in English. He rubbed his

blocky, smoothly shaved chin and looked through the window into the night as though, George guessed, Paco recalled some battle scene of three decades earlier.

"*Sí*," Agripina told George. "In books. But he has clippings."

Paco said Ernest Hemingway, covering the fighting but also writing fiction about it, attached himself to his unit for a while. And Frank Capa photographed the writer with several soldiers Paco knew, all part of the Army of the East.

He described the crossing of the Río Ebro and how the Republic's soldiers, including international brigades, forced Franco's insurgents out of much of the east and repulsed seven counterattacks before weakening. Franco's forces then pushed the Republicans nearly to the Pyrenees.

"All over," Paco said, again in English. He finished his cigarette.

Agripina asked for the clippings.

Paco swiveled in his chair. From a shelf of books behind his desk he withdrew *Los Cipreses Lloran,* laid it open, and from its center handed to Agripina a packet of cellophane-wrapped newspaper-and-magazine articles. He lit another cigarette and leaned back.

"This is the good part," Agripina said. "By the way, Spaniards put cypresses around their cemeteries. That book means 'the cypresses cry.' Anyway, it's about the whole war, including politics and hates and *facciones* and brother fighting brother. He reads it two times just since I know him.

"These clippings say about the Army of the East, mostly by a *periodista* from Córdoba who saw the fighting. Most got printed before Franco won, and the family of Paco guarded them. A few are from a French magazine interviewing comrades of Paco during the three years they worked in the French vineyards." She smiled at Paco and patted his hand. "He acquired the French articles and guarded them even though *mucho tiempo* passed itself before he could understand them."

Paco commented in Spanish.

"What did he say?" George said.

"That he is not embarrassed because he don't understand what I'm telling." She paraphrased some accounts in English, presented others in awkward word-for-word translations.

George, sipping Kahlúa, listened and nodded:

Paco's promotion to captain for leading his platoon in the capture of an important hill the insurgents held . . . His medal and promotion to major for destroying a machine-gun emplacement blocking his unit's advance . . . Paco's three sprints into no-man's-land and rescue of three wounded comrades . . . His promotion to colonel . . . Using grenades and rifle fire to destroy three more machine-gun emplacements . . . Additional awards of medals . . . Helping residents of Barcelona prepare their city for the inevitable attack from Franco . . . Comrades referring to Paco, because of his defiant exploits and apt leadership, as the Army of the East.

"Lots of valuable information," George said. *I've hit the jackpot.*

With the end of the fighting Paco and numberless other Spaniards, to escape reprisals, fled through the Pyrenees to France, where they obtained work, principally in the fields. Paco could exchange mail with his family for the first time in three years. Then Mexico began accepting many of the Republicans, and he obtained ocean passage to Veracruz.

"Franco recently allows them to return," Agripina said, "after all this time."

"Has he gone back?"

"No. Says he will not go unless he lives more than Franco. Many of his family have visited him in Mexico. He married a Mexican and they had good businesses in the capital. You know how Spaniards are. They have grown sons. His wife died. Paco started seeing Mexico along the Pacific Coast: Acapulco, Ixtapa, Zihuatanejo, Manzanillo, San Blas, Mazatlán.

"I tell him he goes from being the Army of the East to the Rooster of the Coast."

George noticed Agripina and Paco smiling at one another.

"He settled here a few years back. That's about it. Any questions?"

"Probably. Can we do this again?"

"I would think so, Jorge Paz."

George and Paco shook hands. "Thank you, Colonel." George turned to Agripina. "Walk you home?"

"Paco will do that after we finish our business."

Again George saw them smiling at each other. "Gotcha." He nodded to Paco, thanked Agripina, and stepped outside. George walked to the front of the building. He stood under the palms and studied the waves for a long time before climbing the stairs to his room.

A couple of days later, still reminiscing about what Don Paco with Agripina's help had told him, and inwardly thanking them, George heard his name when he walked through the shade of the royal poincianas in the central plaza. His name had been shouted several times before he realized it, because of concentrating so on his thoughts. George stopped, turned, saw Stanley Simpson hailing him.

"Where you headed?" Stanley caught up with him.

"To the Océano for a sunset drink."

"Alone?"

"Yes."

"I bet. Blonde, brunette, or redhead? I'll go with you."

Oh, no. "Some other time, Stanley. You see I . . . I'm in the middle of . . . I've got so much thinking to do. I hope you understand."

A Smart Old Bird

George Pease, wearing shorts, Hawaiian shirt, huaraches, and a field worker's straw hat, climbed the wooden stairs at the west end of the Hotel Delicias and paused on the landing to look through the coconut palms to the grand bay and lowering sun. He did this even though he had just paused at the bottom of the stairs to study the same view.

George liked the scratching of sand on the landing as he shifted his feet, heard a different kind of scratching when he rubbed his chin because it itched, noted the squeal of a frigate bird high over the palms as that great soaring, swooping creature hunted for snacks in the shallow water close to shore. He enjoyed watching several breakers finish their journey on the cobblestones and sand in front of the two-story wooden hotel, and he inhaled the sea breeze all the way to his lower ribs, exhaled, nodded.

Momentarily satisfied, as though refueled, George entered his room and hung his hat on the chair by the window. From there he could see beyond the palms and farther up the beach to his right where pelicans just offshore scouted for fish, extended long neck and beak, and dived acrobatically on their targets. He sat there often, musing, thoroughly entertained. But now he had something he wanted the guest across the hall to know.

George removed his flask from the top drawer of the dresser, unscrewed the cap, sipped, returned the cap, put the flask into his pants pocket, crossed the hall, and stepped through the open doorway. From the side of the bed he dragged a chair to the window and sat.

The occupant, Stanley Simpson, leaned out the bathroom doorway, looked at him, disappeared again. "Make yourself comfy, George."

"I detect the sarcasm. Door stood open. Hurry up. I want to show you something." George watched the bay and, off key and out of time, softly hummed *Cielito Lindo*, stopped, sipped from his flask. "Stan?" George addressed the open window, the bay, the late-afternoon breeze, the sand, the rocks, the fish always out of sight, and the closest hunting, diving pelicans he couldn't see because the palms obscured them. But he knew they were there.

"I gotta finish dressing, George."

"This is much more important. Really, really important." George propped a foot on the window sill, leaned back. "You see, Stan, this afternoon I decided I'm a misfit. And so are you and so is everyone like me and you."

"Okay, everyone's a misfit." Stanley sat on the edge of his bed and began putting on sneakers. "I thought you wanted me to see something."

George watched the water, diminished and subjugated by the low sun, the stripe of gleam from that sun receding between waves barely qualifying as breakers. The seashore. He thought the term sounded better in Spanish, *la orilla del mar*. "Where you going?"

"The Océano for a change. You've been telling me the food's good."

George proffered his flask. "And the view. Have a pre-prandial drink."

"I'll have one there. And what are you doing? You're not supposed to drink."

"What are you talking about? Everyone's supposed to drink. It's one of life's great privileges."

"You know what I'm talking about. When you showed off the wallet photos of your son and daughter the other day I saw your AA card. Also your maritime union card and driver's license. What else would you like to know about yourself?"

"Caught me. Anyway, I'm just sipping easy. Come over here and look out this window and up the beach to the north."

Stanley stood behind George and looked where the older man pointed. "I see pelicans diving for sardines."

"Anchovies. Must be a school the way the water's churning. What else do you see?"

"Carne asada with beans and rice, guacamole on the side."

George pointed with added emphasis. "Near where the stream the folks around here call a river empties into the bay. He's on a rise where the path turns up toward the footbridge. See?"

"I don't see anybody."

"Not an 'anybody.' A pelican, a big fellow standing there alone, looking out to the bay, toward the sea. He's got everything figured out. Now he's thinking about it."

"Probably he had all he wants to eat and now he's resting."

"No, Stan. I just told you what he's doing. You see, he's one smart hombre, and he's getting ready to watch his last sunset."

"How long have you been drinking?"

"Since I was sixteen."

"I mean today."

George waved off Stanley's question. "That fellow out there has learned only a few things, compared to you and me. But he learned them well. I can do a lot of things. I can make the freighter go again when it stops running in the middle of the ocean, any freighter, any ship, any ocean. Twenty-seven years I've been going to sea, all my adult life, and I can do plenty around a ship. But I can't do anything as well as that old-timer can perform his few skills. I bet he's smarter than any bird you can name. I mean, plenty of birds can fly."

"Come on, George."

"Not all, but most. And none can fly better than a pelican and most not anywhere near as well. And he can glide and he can fish and he can float. And he has eyes like a buzzard. On top of that, my friend, a pelican even knows when he's going to die. He usually gets enough warning, sometimes just about to the very minute, so he can find a good spot. That big old guy is going to cash in pretty soon. He knows it, so he's come in to the land where he can get warm and relax and find a nice place and not clutter up the water when he goes. The ocean has been good to him. He's not going to pollute it."

"Lots of animals know when they're going to die."

"Not like pelicans know it. Let's have a sip." George offered his flask to Stanley, who refused it. George said, "Don't mind if I do." He sipped, held the flask in his lap, and watched the pelican.

"He looks healthy to me," Stanley said. "I bet he got waterlogged and is just drying out."

"Nope. That's not a resting place. People walk near there all the time, but he's far enough up on land to not be bothered. That's his place. Exclusive. He's got a full belly and he's said good-bye to family and friends, and he's chosen his spot. He's lucky and he's smart. I bet he'd been a pelican before too, and he'll choose the same again. It's a good life, and it's not going to be changed by any politician or too many people talking too much and too loud."

Stanley removed a light jacket from his closet, returned to George's side.

"A pelican is also a beautiful bird," George said. "Ever watch them skim along the water? Usually they fly parallel to shore near a swell or the crest of a wave. It looks like the wave is bringing them in because it's breaking behind them. Once in a while they flap those huge wings but mostly they glide. They rock a little and the wing tips almost touch the water. And sometimes when you're swimming out there one will fly so close you can see his eyeballs roll and watch him looking for fish, cocking his head a little. He's just scouting, though. I've never seen one enter the water when they're flying that low and fast. They're just going somewhere, maybe to those big rocks to the south to rest or sleep or make love.

"When a pelican is hunting he climbs twenty feet, thirty, maybe as much as ninety, and hovers there angling that wise old head, looking for prey, like a submarine periscope would do if it moved along high above the water."

"Come with me, George. The walk will do you good."

"Where you going?"

"I told you. The Océano."

"I've been going there for years. Good food. Nice view of the water."

"You've mentioned that."

"Went there earlier today. They ran me out."

"Kicked you out?"

"I got kicked out of a bar in Marseilles once. No. The noise. Talking, shouting to one another, while I was in need of silence and stars. But too much was said and too loud. That chased me out. Look. He's shifting his position a little."

Stanley looked at the grounded pelican and stepped to the door.

"Ever see one get swamped by a wave, Stan, even when they're flying low like that?"

"No. We didn't have pelicans where I'm from. George, I'm leaving now."

"Of course you haven't seen it because it never happens. If a wave catches up with one it just carries him toward shore and the pelican starts flapping those powerful wings and flinging water every which way and paddling with his duck's feet and pretty soon he's like one of those early airplanes taking off. Mighty entertaining.

"And watching one dive in from high up is beautiful. He'll sort of twist and look and maybe even change direction a little at the last minute before stretching that neck longer than his body and pointing his beak like a spear."

George sipped from his flask. "The fellow's an expert, a genius. Not only is he the best fisherman in the world he's artistic at it too. You could say he's ignorant because he doesn't know much, but you have to figure he's smart because he's so good at what he does know. And most of the fish a pelican is after aren't very big, so imagine what great eyesight he has. And he can continue diving for a long time after sunset."

"The water's clear around here."

"Not all the time. Some days you can't see your feet when you tread water. Think how it would be from high up."

"I'll never know."

"You bet you won't because you're no pelican. And if I had anything to say about it I wouldn't let you be a pelican even if you could see good enough."

"Please shut my door when you leave."

"I'm not going anywhere."

"But if you do, like maybe to your own room."

George watched the bird waddle two steps, stop, and settle onto its belly. "I've always liked pelicans. Not just how magnificently they fly but the way they fish. In college I drove a tour bus weekends at the zoo one summer. When we'd reach the pelican cage I used to say, 'There's Mr. Pelican. Holds more in his beak than his belly can.' Everyone would laugh, every time, kids and grownups too. Imagine caging a pelican. They don't do that anymore, just clip the wings. They make good pets. Don't let one sit on your lap, however.

"Sometimes one bus would draw closer to the next than we normally drove, and if you could hear everyone on the other bus laughing you knew they were at the pelican cage. All the drivers said it. I said it six times a day for two days a week, and I still laughed. And I still like to watch pelicans."

Stanley stood on the top landing.

George saw the long beak swing when the pelican nodded, stretched its wings, and refolded them.

"In the first place, George, the Mexicans might call that bird a pelican, but I don't. It obviously doesn't have a sack under its beak that holds more than its belly can, as you put it."

"Does."

"Doesn't."

"I suppose you think he's an oversized sea gull."

"Maybe. I can't get a good look from here. Doesn't have a long neck either."

"Watch those diving just beyond the swells. If they come up with a fish, or lots of little ones, you can see the sack hanging under the beak."

"I've seen them every day I've been here."

"Maybe you looked but didn't see. I wish I were half as smart as that pelican. This is his last sunset and he knows it. This is his land and his sea. You and me, we don't fit in the States, and so we come here, interlopers. But we don't fit here either."

"See you later."

George listened to Stanley descend the stairs and watched him follow the path connecting with the center of town. When it turned upstream toward the footbridge Stanley turned with it and soon moved out of George's sight. *Didn't even glance at the old pelican. Did I expect him to?*

Moving to his own room, he sat by the window, sipped from his flask, and watched the pelican on the slight rise near the mouth of the stream. *He can watch his friends and family out there flying and diving and he can have his own thoughts and his own sunset, same as me.*

The sun, turning orange, began disappearing at the horizon. The sea looked blue and green, and the western half of the sky turned gray except where slender clouds spread through it horizontally, reflecting orange and red and green and pink. George knew that when he could no longer see the sun the clouds overhead and behind him would turn pink. *This is one of the best sunsets I've ever seen. I'm sure that pelican appreciates it as much as I do.*

George sat at his window a long time. He watched until he could no longer see the old pelican, and the other birds quit fishing, and he toasted the sea, the sunset, and all pelicans. *I was in need of silence and stars, and too much was said, too loud.*

The cleaning girl's scream awakened Stanley Simpson the next morning. He slipped on his pants and jerked open his door to find the girl standing in George's open doorway, hands to her mouth, back to the room. Stan stepped past her, saw the man slumped in his chair by his window. Stan thought he slept. But when he touched George's shoulder he knew George had died.

Stanley told the girl to contact the hotel owner, who lived downstairs in the back. He returned to his own room, donned a shirt, and hurried down the stairs. Along the path connecting with the center of town Stanley walked with hands in pockets, head bowed, trying to erase the image in George's room.

He didn't notice when the path turned, soon found himself about to step on the sprawled body of a pelican. He stopped, saw wing feathers long and thin, some broken, noted gaps where others had been. The bird seemed much larger than Stanley had estimated the day before.

With his bare foot he lifted the corpse to see it better, though he found this more unsettling than touching George's shoulder with his hand a few minutes earlier. The dead pelican rolled, and the huge distensible gular pouch, now relaxed under the beak, flopped onto the sand. The bird's neck seemed as long as its body.

Stanley thought for a moment the sea had hushed, that the breeze had died. He walked into the water until a foamy wave soaked far up his pants legs.

He couldn't remember which foot he touched the pelican with, so he wriggled both into the sand, strained to dig them in.

A Cold Night

◇◇◇◇◇◇◇◇◇◇◇◇◇◇◇◇◇◇◇◇◇◇◇◇◇◇◇◇◇◇◇◇

Mike had told Valerie he didn't want to sit within range of anyone's voice except hers. But when the manager led them to an unoccupied table by the fireplace they sat because of the cold night even though two couples occupied a table nearby.

"We can pretend we're alone," Valerie whispered.

"They're already eating. Maybe they'll leave soon."

So they sat in the small dining room at Rancho La Gloria, watched the flames and chatted while examining the menu. From a radio in the kitchen they could hear the news in Spanish, though not clearly enough for Valerie to understand.

And a woman at the table closest to them, the eldest of the two women, talked so much that Mike's mood, already saturnine, worsened. He looked at her, grumbled, studied the flames.

Valerie saw Mike's scowl, caught his tone. "If you'd had a better day at Caliente you wouldn't even hear her."

"I know, but I didn't. And I'm a poor loser."

She smiled and placed her hand on his knee. "You are not. Usually." She removed her coat. "The fire's great."

"But listen to her. We shouldn't have to hear all this even if I'd finally won a race."

"Should we drive on to Rosarito Beach? It'll be warm in the car."

"No. I'm too hungry, and so are you." He removed his coat.

So they watched the fire and chatted until the waiter, tall and thin in white dress shirt and black pants, arrived.

"I am Xicoténcatl," he said. "Call me Xico." He smiled and waited.

They ordered tequila sours and the carne asada dinners, and Xico left.

And Valerie resumed trying to help Mike soften and to ignore the woman's comments.

"She's a living travelogue," he said.

"Shhh. She'll hear."

"Except for the night life," the woman told her companions, "forget Buenos Aires. The best steaks and wines are in Montevideo. Less expensive too. And better nearby beaches."

Mike frowned at the flames.

"But maybe she's right," Valerie whispered.

"Maybe. But it's the way she says it."

Valerie judged the woman to be in her early forties, saw her as pretty, with a good figure, heard her friends call her Justine. Valerie wondered about the true color of Justine's hair, dark brown with auburn tints, and she liked it, the woman's brown eyes too, though she felt they possessed a sorrow or a longing. Justine frequently sipped her cocktail. The other couple and Justine's escort seemed to be in their early twenties, like Valerie and Mike.

"Why don't those two guys join the conversation?" Mike said. "They might have been to war or traveled all over, or maybe they play professional sports. They probably have plenty to talk about."

"Don't forget the other woman." Valerie poked his arm. "She might be an Olympic champion or a movie star."

"I get your point."

"And I yours."

"But, Val, you shouldn't be so logical. Did you forget we're in Mexico?"

Xico brought their drinks. From blending, a thin layer of foam topped each.

Mike nodded toward the kitchen. "Anything in the news we should know?"

"Not much new. Your Senator Kennedy looks more presidential every day."

"He's running, all right."

"Meanwhile I still like Ike. I'll turn the radio off when the guitarist arrives."

Valerie and Mike clinked glasses, sipped, and discussed their afternoon at the Thoroughbred races in nearby Tijuana.

"I know," Valerie said. "You don't want to talk about it because you lost every race you bet. Every single race. Just imagine that." Her smile teased.

"I recall."

"But weren't the horses beautiful?"

"Yours were."

They often chose Rancho La Gloria for a good meal after the horse races or a bullfight in Tijuana, liked its rural setting, intimacy, the tables and chairs of dark wood, wrought-iron wall lamps and Tiffany-style lamps overhead. They admired the paintings of Mexican landscapes and reconstructed archaeological sites and always enjoyed the music, soft, romantic.

The radio went silent. A guitarist at the other end of the room began playing and singing *En Mi Viejo San Juan*.

"It's special here," Valerie said. "This is our place."

"Agreed. If only—" He nodded toward Justine.

"You mean La Perla," Justine said. "The Mirador is the hotel. But the restaurant where you sit to watch the cliff divers is La Perla. Very commercial of course. But when you're in Acapulco you don't want to miss it. And don't be deceived when they throw a rope into the water and the diver seems to go for it desperately. They always toss it just as the surge is taking the diver out. But the next wave would bring him back anyway. The rope is actually to help the young man climb back up the rocks. But they're brave and daring. It's quite a good stunt."

Her listeners nodded, and the younger woman smiled over her glass of wine.

Valerie felt she could hear Mike grinding his teeth while staring at his drink. She kissed him on the ear and whispered, "I know. It's the way she says it."

Mike smiled.

"That's better."

"We know her name," Mike said. "Let's name the others. Maybe that'll help. The girl's a blue-eyed blonde like you. Perhaps also a Swede. She could be Valerie II."

"No, she couldn't. How about Greta Garbo or Ingrid Bergman? They're Swedes too."

"I choose Ingrid. Her date with his bow tie looks like a master of ceremonies."

"How about Ed Sullivan?" Valerie said.

"Good. Now for Other Guy."

"Let's wait. Here comes our food. I smell the steaks already."

Xico served their carne asada dinners. Valerie and Mike ordered Chenin Blanc by L. A. Cetto. Xico made a note and stepped to the nearby table where Justine had started telling about her second husband: handsome and intelligent, wealthy and cultured, educated and charismatic.

"That must make the man she's with feel great," Mike said. "Why doesn't she have his virtues tattooed on her arm? Her friends have more patience than a turtle." He loaded meat and guacamole onto his fork, and when he started the fork toward his mouth the morsel tumbled onto his plate.

He jabbed the escaped bite with his fork and put it into his mouth.

Justine commented about owning a European-made automobile Valerie recognized as expensive, and she saw Mike frown at the fire.

"You'll ruin your meal," Valerie said.

"But how can her boyfriend or husband or whatever stand her? I can't, and I'm just a suffering spectator. And we forgot to name him."

"Perhaps she isn't that way when you get to know her."

Mike smiled for the second time since they sat. "I think you could love a baboon."

"I already do."

He tipped his wine glass toward her.

The guitarist began playing and singing *Creí*.

"Do you know the words?"

"He believed her life was his," Valerie said, "that she loved him like he loved her."

Justine told about some of Tijuana's often-missed attractions. "Be sure to try the paella *valenciana* at Chiki Jai. And check out the Club BIC and the art gallery under it. And there're the Foreign Club and Caesar's restaurant and the good shops nearby."

"Now," Mike said, "she's also an expert on Tijuana."

"She seems to have traveled a lot."

"Thank you so much."

"It's just possible he loves her, you know."

"But how can she—?"

"You'll just have to ignore her."

"I've been trying to."

"Please try again." Valerie patted his leg.

Justine announced so many things with such effusive gestures and expressions that Valerie knew Mike couldn't ignore her. And Justine's companions listened and nodded and smiled, offering brief comments. When Xico cleared their table they ordered Kahlúa. Justine and both men brought out cigarettes, and the men competed to light Justine's.

Valerie guessed that Justine's talking binge owed itself to loneliness, despite her company, and perhaps to too many cocktails.

Xico cleared the foursome's table, left, and returned with their check.

"Olé," Mike told the fireplace.

But only the two men and the younger woman stood. And while Sullivan put money on the waiter's bill tray, and Other Guy placed money on the table, Ingrid offered her hand to Justine. "I'm so glad to have met you."

Justine stood. "Me too," and they hugged.

"I wished we'd met you sooner," Sullivan said.

"Oh, so do I," she told him, and they hugged. "Don't let one of those big rockets go astray and take you off to Mars." Justine kissed his cheek. They hugged again.

"I'll guard your address and phone number like a Sunday," Other Guy said. "And you know how to find me. Let's get together soon."

"Oh, how I hope so," Justine told him. They kissed and embraced.

The younger trio left. Valerie saw Justine watch their exit. When they stepped out of the restaurant Justine sat and sipped her drink, snatched up the pack of cigarettes from the table, removed one and put it between her lips. She grabbed her lighter, spun the wheel three times though it flamed on the second, and put the flame to the cigarette, first in the middle, then on the end. Justine extinguished it after one puff.

"Interesting," Mike whispered to Valerie. "She just met those others."

"And now she seems to be waiting for someone."

Valerie watched while Justine glanced at the flaming

logs in the fireplace, examined other diners, grabbed her cigarette package again, and shook some of its contents onto the table. She picked one up, dropped it, captured it, and put it between her lips. Her lighter worked on first try, and she held its flame on the end too long. Justine inhaled and exhaled, rested the cigarette in the ashtray, and finished her Kahlúa in one swallow. She looked around, caught the waiter's attention. When Xico reached her table Justine ordered a double shot of Chivas Regal.

"Sad." Valerie thought she saw Justine shiver.

Justine reached behind her and pulled her coat over her shoulders. She picked up her cigarette with one hand, tapped the table top with the other, stared at the fireplace.

Valerie watched the fire and sipped her wine. *The poor woman. Who is she? Where is she from? How is she getting home? Or is she lodged here?* Valerie looked at Mike, who watched the burning logs. She couldn't read his expression. *Is Mike lamenting his losses at the track? Rehashing his irritation with Justine? Searching for something in the fire?*

Mike nodded at the flames before facing Valerie.

Again she couldn't read his expression. But she saw a small crooked smile.

Mike stood.

He stepped to Justine's side.

"Come join us," Mike said.

LUPE

◇◇◇◇◇◇◇◇◇◇

"How are you doing up there, Carlitos?"
"Fine, Mama."
"Watch your balance."
"Okay. Will we do good today?"
"With that smile of yours? Of course, Champ." Lupe pedaled the unicycle on the sidewalk between the Parque Alameda and Avenida Juárez, rolled off the walkway at a low curb and onto the street, pausing in a taxi stand. She set her feet onto the pavement, lifted the boy from her shoulders, and stood him beside her.

On the opposite side of the avenue in a grand half-circle monument reigned the seated likeness of Benito Juárez, who led Mexico to independence from foreign rule.

"We'll rest a bit before working."

Guadalupe María Estudillo, called Lupe, and her four-year-old son, Rodrigo Carlos, had become common sights at some of the busy intersections and tourist attractions in vast and varied Mexico City, crowded and hurried, even madcap at times, yet alluring.

Almost daily mother and child mined tips from the city's harried motorists and pedestrians, Lupe pedaling a unicycle, Carlitos mounted on her shoulders, Lupe's ponytail pinned on top of her head, each in shorts, sneakers, and shirt. Carlitos offered his child-size wide-brimmed sombrero as receptacle for contributions, the coins and paper money welcomed equally. With his other hand he waved a Mexican flag.

The unicycle lacked handlebars. It comprised pedals, a bicycle wheel, and a high seat. If Carlitos could not lean over far enough to accept a gratuity, Lupe took it with either hand.

When mother and son performed their exhibition in an open space like the big flagstone ramp in front of the Palacio de Bellas Artes, or on the magnificent central plaza known as the Zócalo, men, women, and children paused to watch and applaud their singular balancing act:

Lupe racing the unicycle, then braking and turning a circle as though on a centavo, or making a half-circle on the same metaphorical coin; spinning the vehicle once, twice, three times; sending it backwards with equal skill; and executing each maneuver while on her shoulders Carlitos sat smiling and waving his hat and flag.

At an important intersection, numberless in the metropolis, the whirling-and-balancing act assumed the added characteristic of haste and daring: Even though the performers could be enjoying the protection of a red traffic signal, motorists often ignored such electronic instructions, Lupe's caution, therefore, constantly paramount.

"How did you do today, Lupita?"

"About the same, Mama: the subway in each direction crowded like a stack of tortillas, passersby watching with interest but not always giving, smog oppressive, people honking horns and yelling at one another, women drivers as rude as men." Lupe slipped out of her shorts and pulled on jeans. "I felt we'd get rained on."

Rodrigo Carlos, carrying a soccer ball and still wearing

his "work clothes," exited the bedroom. "Can I go out and play?" He spoke to the enchiladas his grandmother prepared.

"No," Lupe said.

"Yes," his grandmother, Arabela, told him.

The women laughed.

Carlitos looked from one to the other.

"Go ahead, Champ," Lupe said. "But we eat soon. Stay in shouting distance."

"That's easy." He started for the door.

"Don't let the big kids steal your soccer ball." Arabela watched him leave. "He's a spirited little guy. His grandfather would have cherished that child."

Lupe nodded, stepped to her mother's side and began making an enchilada. "Carlitos would be in the circus with him by now."

"You and your son have your own circus."

"He has wonderful balance. Mama, Papa's been gone a long time. Why don't you remarry?"

"Not interested. And anyone I meet in this barrio would be at least a burglar or an armed robber. You know that."

"You're still youthful, trim, not a gray hair. Give up sales at the store and work at one of the big hotels. You'll meet someone."

"Hah." Arabela dropped meatballs into the soup.

"I got three more marriage proposals today, Mama."

"What did you tell them?"

Lupe laughed. "'Not interested.'" She looked through the kitchen window to the street, narrow, pavement broken, gutters littered with trash. Lupe heard her son's laughter and shouting while he played with friends. *But I am interested, just not in the men I meet.* "I don't want to make another mistake, Mama. You know that. I need a real job, though." *But for now Carlitos needs to be with me. Imagine leaving him unguarded or even with another family in this part of the city. And he can't go with my mother to her work.*

"I said we're out of meatballs."

"Sorry, Mama. Daydreaming."

"I know."

"I'll go buy some ground round."

"We're all right for tonight. Tomorrow I'll go to the market anyway. Come with me. You and Carlitos aren't going to work with your unicycle, are you?"

"We'll go to the market and to Mass with you. I want to wear my good dress. And let's buy an *Excélsior* so I can read the funnies to Carlitos. But around midafternoon I'm going to find a good spot near Plaza Garibaldi. On Sunday there's bound to be a lot of traffic there."

"Yes, until dawn, probably. Be careful. You know that area's reputation."

"We'll be home before dark, Mama."

Lupe heard the music long before she could see the arch identifying Plaza de Garibaldi, the square a long-time gathering place for mariachi groups from throughout the city. It thrived a few blocks north of the Palacio de Bellas Artes, carried the name of an Italian soldier of fortune. Now some mariachis entertained in the cantinas and restaurants framing three sides of the plaza. Others mingled at the curb or throughout the square, waiting for motorists to stop and hire them for significant events, especially birthdays and weddings.

"I hear music, Mama. Is that where we're going?" Carlitos pointed.

"That's it," Lupe told the boy riding her shoulders. "You can get down if you see a girl your age and want to dance a little, like you do sometimes with the TV."

"Why would I want to dance with a girl?"

Lupe patted his leg. "All right. I won't insist. Besides, I hope we'll be too busy." She swerved the unicycle to avoid a couple running across the street, and she rolled to the curb, stopping between cars carrying men waving to attract the attention of mariachis nearby. She set Carlitos onto the pavement and dismounted and headed for the kiosk in the center of the plaza, where they sat on a wrought-iron bench, the unicyle leaning against the kiosk and connected to Lupe's wrist by a sturdy leather leash.

"Mama, they're not all playing the same song."

"Doesn't seem to matter. Look. See the statues?" Lupe pointed to the life-size bronzes nearby. "Great singers, all of them." She named them: Jorge Negrete, Pedro Infante, Javier Solís.

"Let's get one of my father and put it there."

Lupe placed an arm around him. "But he didn't sing, Champ. This place is only for singers and musicians."

"I bet he could be a singer."

"Could have been. Yes, perhaps."

"Maybe we could put one of him somewhere else."

"We can give that some thought." Lupe patted his shoulder, studied the passersby: couples and men alone, an occasional young woman hurrying along in a swirling, flowery long dress, and, singly and in small groups, mariachis hatted or not in boots and tight-fitting pants and bolero jackets, black or gray or brown, conchos glistening, frilly white shirts, and string ties. Some carried holstered pistols on their hips.

"This place is fun," Carlitos said.

"Yes. There didn't used to be anything here. Grandmother says the first mariachis came down from a little town in Jalisco a long time ago, and this is what happened."

From various directions the music—from brass, violins, and guitars—flowed without end. Lupe tapped her foot to *Son de la Negra* bursting from a nearby cantina. But when *Gema* escaped from an even-closer establishment she gave up.

Rodrigo Carlos, she noted, tapped in confusion. In a moment he looked at her and smiled, also in confusion.

Lupe laughed. "Ready to work, Champ? We can hear just as well from the sidewalk and earn a few pesos too."

"Sure, Mama."

"Just don't fall off trying to keep time to two tunes at once." Lupe steadied herself with one hand on the side of the kiosk to mount her unicycle, then pulled her son up until he could climb onto her shoulders.

Rolling past men and women who looked at mother and son in surprise, dodging others who almost walked into them, and waving to mariachis who saluted them, Lupe and her agile assistant glided to the sidewalk to claim a spot on the north rim of Plaza de Garibaldi.

Observers gathered, applauding Lupe's maneuvers on her contraption, some dropping coins into Carlitos's hat. After a while Lupe had decided to rest when a black Mercedes sedan stopped opposite them, and the driver watched her. She moved her feet from pedals to sidewalk and helped Carlitos descend.

"That's quite a stunt you two have." The driver leaned his head out the window.

"It's a living," Lupe said. *Actually not so much.*

"Takes a lot of guts."

Lupe shrugged, noted his youth, tieless white silk shirt, his car common among upper-class Mexicans. She liked his thin mustache resembling Javier Solís's, enjoyed his coruscating smile.

"I've seen you before," he said.

"I've never been here before."

"No, I mean at some intersection, or maybe on the Zócalo."

"Maybe." Lupe put her foot on a pedal. "We have to get back to work."

"Wait-wait. Can't we talk a minute?"

"You should get going too. You're parked on the wrong side of the street."

"Hey, this is Mexico." He waved a hand in disdain. "Send the boy to his nanny and let's have a glass of wine."

"No sale." Lupe mounted her unicycle and rolled to a nearby streetlamp, where with one hand she steadied herself against the lamppost while helping Carlitos onto her shoulders.

"Wait for me at the kiosk," the man called out.

Lupe looked at the red lights of a police motorcycle stopping behind his car. "I don't think you have time."

"What do you mean?"

"You have to go to jail first." She watched him look into his rearview mirror and grimace. Lupe and Carlitos rolled away.

"Where to, Mama?"

"Just to the other side of the plaza. Tips have been good."

"Are you mad at that man?"

"No, but he doesn't have anything else to do. We do."

"I liked him."

"If we see him again you do the talking."

They sat once more on the bench by the kiosk, the unicycle leaning against it and leashed to Lupe's wrist. More mariachis had arrived. Automobiles almost in tandem stopped at the curb, hiring musicians or not, and rolling on. Every cantina, it seemed to Lupe, blasted music into the afternoon.

"We can do one more session." Lupe glanced at the sun. "Then we hurry home."

"We did good today, didn't we?"

"Yes. Would you like to come here every Sunday?"

"You bet. Can we count our money now?"

"Oh, Champ, no. This place is full of people we have to be careful about. We keep our money in our pockets and don't let anyone bump into us. Besides, we're not through work."

They stood by the bench, and Lupe had unfastened her unicycle's leash and tied it around her waist when he approached.

"I had hoped you'd be here," he said.

"We have to rest somewhere once in a while."

"Of course. Let's start over. I'm Francisco Toledo." He extended his hand.

Lupe hesitated, one hand supporting the unicycle, saw his smile. *It's brightening the plaza despite the daylight.* She took his proffered hand, quickly released it. "Guadalupe María Estudillo. Lupe." She placed her hand on Carlitos's shoulder. "My son, Rodrigo Carlos."

The boy shook the man's hand.

"Call me Paco," Francisco Toledo told him, then addressed Lupe. "Can we sit? Can we talk?"

Lupe again hesitated, felt Carlitos tugging her hand. *Does Carlitos want us to sit or to go?* Another tug. *To sit.* "For a few minutes. Then we need to get back to work."

They sat on the bench.

Lupe unpinned her ponytail, let it flow black and silken down her back. "They didn't hold you in jail very long."

"Didn't even take me. Mexico, remember?" He laughed, rubbed thumb and forefinger together, the bribery symbol Lupe had known all her life and occasionally invoked, the *mordida*. "Your hair looks better this way."

Lupe shrugged. "It gets in my son's way if I don't pin it up."

They discussed the overcast sky, the raucous traffic, the unending music. When Paco asked her a personal question Lupe gave a vague answer—or none.

After a lull in their conversation he began offering information about himself: He worked in finance, was born in Houston. "My parents felt medical care would be better there." Paco worked mainly in Mexico City and important provincial capitals. "I travel a lot." He had homes in Acapulco and Cancún. "Not Huatulco, though. Artificial."

Lupe took mental notes. *I don't care how artificial. I'd still like to see it. The other places too. Anywhere.*

And they watched mariachis walking past and playing tunes or warming up, saw the young women in folkloric costume hurrying to one of the larger cantinas.

"Dancers." Paco motioned in their direction. "It's a good show. Want to catch it?"

"Yes," Carlitos said.

"Not today." Lupe stood.

Paco stood. "It's too noisy here anyway for talking. Let's go somewhere else. Maybe you're hungry. How about it?"

"I'm starving," Carlitos said.

"We're working, Champ."

"Are you certain you have to go?" Paco said. "The evening hasn't begun."

"Quite certain. Besides, I'm not dressed for going out, and I need to get my son home. *Am I vacillating? Did I give him an opening?*" She pinned up her ponytail.

"There are places we can go. You're beautiful just as you are."

She saw him look at her legs, little more than a glance, but she noted his approval. Lupe stood on the bench and mounted the one-wheeler. When she reached for her son, Paco lifted Carlitos onto her shoulders. She thanked him.

"Hands free. I don't see how you do it. That one-wheeler scares me."

Paco's bright flashing smile told her otherwise.

"How can I see you again?" he said. "Where can I find you?"

"The craziest intersections. The Zócalo. Chapultepec Park. Wave good-bye to the gentleman, Carlitos." Lupe again pedaled them to the sidewalk on the south rim of Plaza de Garibaldi. And as she went through her routines, and Carlitos collected tips, Lupe looked around occasionally to see if Francisco Toledo stood nearby. Though she never spotted him, she felt certain he would find her. *But I'm not sure I want him to.*

At home they finished their desserts of custard and set their bowls aside. Carlitos had consumed two portions. Lupe smiled at him.

Arabela nodded at his empty bowl. "Does that mean you liked it, Carlitos?"

"Yes, Grandma. Mamma, can I go play?"

"Yes, but it'll be dark soon. Stay close."

"Now, Lupe," Arabela said when Carlitos ran outside, "who is this Paco your son has been promoting ever since the two of you walked in the door?"

"Oh, Mama, just another flirt."

"One of your many marriage proposals on this day?"

"No. I did get four, however."

"We should make a mark on the wall for each one. So that's why he's special? He wouldn't propose?"

"He's not special. Oh, maybe a little. He's likable. Oh, he admired my legs."

"I'm not surprised. You could win a leg competition anytime, make the movie stars and TV queens look like theirs are spaghetti."

Lupe told of Paco Toledo's work, his car, homes in two resort towns.

"Lupita, Acapulco? I bet he's a crook. Acapulco's got crooks like maggots on a mule carcass." Arabela started to clear the table.

"I've had the same thought." Lupe stood, carried dishes to the sink. "Our barrio's full of criminals too."

"But they're ours, not heinous killers like in the drug trade. Is he married?"

"He didn't say and I didn't ask."

"Why not? You sound interested. Did he ask you out?"

"Yes. I'm not going." Lupe gathered more soiled dishes.

"Why not? You haven't gone out with anyone in a long time."

"Haven't met anyone I wanted to spend time with."

"Until now, I'd say."

Lupe began drying dishes while her mother washed. "Mama, when he finds out we live in Tepito he won't want to see me."

"Meet him at Parque Alameda."

"Mama, I don't have anything to wear."

"What's wrong with your blue dress? The red one?"

"You know what I mean." Lupe gave her mother a feeble smile.

"So where are you going to see him again?"

"I told him some of the main places Carlitos and I go."

"You're not trying very hard, Lupita."

Throughout Mexico, cities, towns, even villages, often refer to their central square as the Zócalo. Most such squares or plazas are actually named, however, for a prominent national or local personage, perhaps for a happening, sometimes for a meaningful date. The central square in Mexico City is officially the Plaza de la Constitución.

Guadalupe María Estudillo often chose it as a place for her and her son to earn some coins. She did so on this afternoon because foot traffic in front of the Palacio de Bellas Artes, her first choice, had been light. Lupe pedaled them along Avenida Juárez and its extension, Calle Madero, and onto the large paving stones of the Zócalo.

After a while she asked Rodrigo Carlos, "Are you about ready for a rest, Champ?"

"Sure, Mama. My hat's getting filled up too."

"So are my pockets." Lupe searched faces as she spun a slow circle. *Good crowd. Some staying around. Others pausing, moving on. No benches. We can sit on the cathedral steps.*

"There he is, Mama." Carlitos pointed and twisted. "Turn again, Mama."

"Who do you mean?"

"Paco. It's Paco." Carlitos shouted and waved.

Lupe examined the back of the crowd, didn't locate him, wished she enjoyed an overview like her son's, continued sending the unicycle through her various maneuvers. *Maybe it's not him. But I could use a rest. And so what if it is Paco?*

In a few moments, applauding, smiling, Francisco Toledo stood at the front of the onlookers. When Lupe started lowering Carlitos, Paco took the boy and set him down.

"Every day," Paco said, "I've looked all over for you."

"I hope you don't lose your job."

He laughed. "Not a chance. Let's sit."

That smile again. "We were heading for the cathedral steps."

"There's a second-story restaurant near the Monte de Piedad." He motioned over his shoulder toward the big pawn shop. "We can see everything, get a bite, have a chat."

"Like this?" Lupe pointed to her shorts, her hair.

"It's informal. Come on. They'll even guard your bike for you. Right, Carlitos?"

"Let's do it, Mama."

Lupe unpinned her ponytail. She took Carlitos's hand.

Paco maneuvered the unicycle.

Tense, fighting to suppress her embarrassment, Lupe climbed upstairs to the restaurant. But she relaxed after looking around: Patrons included several women wearing shorts, and the environment felt friendly, the restaurant, its view of the grand plaza, the Colonial cathedral, and ancient federal government buildings.

She requested a turkey sandwich for herself, one of tuna for Carlitos, iced tea for each. Francisco Toledo ordered a ham-and-cheese sandwich and American-style coffee. Lupe knew an interrogation approached. But she liked him. *I won't be evasive this time. And if I scare him off, so be it.*

"So: How are you and your intrepid helper doing today?"

"The Zócalo is good to us." Lupe nodded toward the plaza. "Considering."

"You could do better. Have you tried modeling? The movies?"

Lupe laughed. "Not this girl. Besides, Carlitos needs to be with me."

"We've made models at home, Mama."

"That's different, Champ. The gentleman means wear fancy clothes to show rich women." She glanced through the window, inhaled deeply, exhaled, faced Paco. "We live with my mother. She has a sales job. After Carlitos starts school I'll look for something."

"I hope you're not married and don't have a boyfriend."

"If I did I wouldn't be here with you. Look, I got married too young. He was too young also, got involved with some scary people while trying to make money on the dark side and got killed two years ago. Are you married? My mother told me to ask."

"No. I'm too young." Paco smiled. "Tell me more. What's with the unicycle?"

The waiter brought their sandwiches, tea, and coffee.

"My father performed in the circus. Tightrope walker and acrobat. I couldn't stay away. I loved the circus. He often took me and my mother along when they traveled. It had a unicycle rider with the clowns, and that one-wheeler fascinated me. My father had a smaller unicycle built for me, and before long I rode it in an act. Ever have people applaud and cheer you?"

"Not hardly."

"The adoration is addictive. Anyway I had the knack and I did well. Then a midair transfer went wrong during my father's trapeze act, and he fell. His momentum carried him beyond the net. Lived for three days before dying. Mama and I soon became penniless, and we'd lost interest in the circus. The only place we could afford to rent was in a barrio. Wound up in Tepito."

"Good Lord!"

"Coyoacán would have been nice. What area do you live in?"

"Polanco."

"I hear it's desirable."

"Yes. I'm lucky."

Carlitos finished his sandwich. "Mama, can I stand by the window over there? It's bigger." Carlitos pointed.

"Just don't forget where we are."

"He's good company." Paco watched Carlitos trot toward the other window.

"Yes. Also very bright. Has terrific coordination, wants his own unicycle. We could form a new act. I prefer the present one. I'm using the second bike I had during my career as child star of the circus." Lupe nodded at the corner where Paco had set her unicycle. "I dusted it off and oiled it recently, raised the seat quite a lot."

"I don't even know if they sell those things anywhere."

"I could have one made for him in Tepito. You can get anything there."

"I've heard. Mostly stolen."

"Some. The Barrio de Tepito has a whole other culture as honest as you are."

"What's going to happen when the boy is too big to ride your shoulders?"

"I'll teach him to be a pickpocket."

Carlitos trotted to the table. "Mama. Paco. The Zócalo is full of Indians."

"Are they shooting bows and arrows?"

"No, Mama. They're standing around with signs."

Paco said, "Those are from Chiapas. They've been

protesting, want the government to help with their problems."

"Which are?"

"Police brutality. Poor roads. Unemployment."

"Oh, like here."

"I'm going back." Carlitos trotted to his former viewing spot.

"Your turn. You said you were in finance. What does that mean?"

"I buy and sell businesses. Develop an occasional vacant lot. I deal with bankers."

"But also you must have money of your own."

"Sure. My father helped me at first." Paco laughed. "Now I help him."

"Where's your office?"

"In the Camino Real Building. I'll show you."

"Never mind. I've seen pictures."

"And my car has a phone."

"Do you have a business card?"

"Just ran out. I'm having more printed."

Lupe examined the plaza. *He sounds honest, doesn't look or act like a crook. Every person with money can't be a criminal. And that smile . . .* "Oh, look. I hate to see that." A young man in the center of the Zócalo leaned his head back, put a bottle to his lips, removed it, pocketed it, spat, and ignited a cigarette lighter in front of his lips. He opened his mouth. Flames shot out and quickly disappeared. He reached for the bottle.

Paco had watched. "That flattened me the first time I saw it."

"My competition for the stray centavo. How tragic."

"Him and the windshield cleaners and car watchers."

"And beggars. We're a quite diverse city."

Carlitos rejoined them. "Did you see that? He keeps fire in his mouth." Her son turned to leave.

Lupe grabbed his arm. "Let's don't watch. Sit here with us."

"But I've never seen anything like that."

"Now you have. Sit here. Want some ice cream? Is that all right, Paco?"

"Can I have strawberry? Later in the Zócalo maybe the fire guy will talk to us."

Carlitos picked up a spoon and looked toward the waiter.

"While you're eating," Lupe said, "would you like a story about this place?"

The boy nodded.

"All right," Lupe told him. "A long time ago Indians from the north known as Aztecas or Mexicas looked for a place to settle down. They got tired of walking, and when they got here and saw an eagle perched on a cactus at the edge of a big lake they made a public square right where this one is and built a city. They named it Tenochtitlán. In the time of their famous chief Moctezuma they called the square the Plaza Mayor. Moctezuma had a huge palace, a beautiful garden, and lots of birds."

"Can we see them later?" His ice cream arrived and he started eating it.

"They're all gone, Champ."

"How come?"

"Some men from a far-off land heard Moctezuma had lots of gold. They decided they wanted it, so they sailed here across the ocean." Lupe noticed Paco smiling at her.

"They had better weapons and horses," she said, "which had never been seen here, and so they took over. They had plenty of help from Indian tribes who didn't like the Aztecas, and lots of people got killed."

"Did those men get the gold?"

"Some."

"And later under a chief named Maximiliano beautiful trees filled the square. But we had a revolution, and the revolutionaries cut down the trees so they could get a better shot at the Palacio Nacional and President Díaz."

"I'm done." Carlitos pushed away his ice cream dish.

"You could teach school," Paco said.

"I have the only student I want."

"Can your mother watch him when we go out?"

"Are we going out?"

"I hope so. What's your address?"

"You're planning to pick me up in Tepito? Just like that?"

"That's the way dates are done nowadays."

"While I'm introducing you to my mother your car's wheels would disappear."

Paco laughed.

"The hood ornament too. And you'd be mistaken for a cop or a politician and maybe get jumped."

"I'll think of an acceptable disguise."

Lupe sat at the kitchen table doodling in one of her son's coloring books. She occasionally looked out the window to the street while her mother chopped up chicken breasts, onions, tomatoes, and other ingredients for tacos. Dough for the shells sat in a small mound on Arabela's left. On her right rested a bowl of jalapeños and another of cilantro. She had fixed her hair, as black as Lupe's, in a bun. While she worked, her back to Lupe, she told of that day's happenings in the Barrio de Tepito.

"We got a truckload of clothing, men's and women's. Of course I didn't ask where it came from . . . A truck also arrived with men's and boys' shoes. I grabbed two pair that should fit Carlitos, one sneakers, the other shiny brown leather, not a scratch. They're in the closet . . . Shortly after I got home the Ventura brothers showed up with a brand new bike for Carlitos."

"How thoughtful."

"I sent them away with it. Too big and too new. Some-one would steal it sure . . . One of our clerks heard about a dead man in the alley behind the flea market . . . A new family moved into the house where the Garcías had been. Know where I mean?"

"Yes, Mama."

"Parents, a grandmother, and four kids in that little two-room shack like ours. How long do you think they can last?"

"Yes, Mama."

Arabela twisted to see Lupe. "You're farther away than Xochimilco. Want to talk while Carlitos is with his friends?"

Lupe pushed the coloring book aside. "Paco asked me out."

"What did you say?"

"I'd let him know tomorrow. You'd have to watch Carlitos."

"That's all right. To dinner? The boy will be asleep."

"Paco mentioned Silvain's, the San Ángel Inn, some others."

"Nice to have a choice. Which would you choose?"

Lupe reached for the book. "The place wouldn't matter to me, and the price wouldn't to him. It's just . . ."

"You still think he might be a gangster? A crook of some sort?"

"That, and I'm attracted to him. I just don't want to make another mistake."

"Lupita, you haven't been out with him even once yet."

Lupe laughed. "I don't have anything to wear."

"Get your dreamy carcass up here and make some tortillas." Arabela made room at the counter for her. "That shipment of clothing that came in today? Some of the women's dresses are top labels. You want Armani? Dolce & Gabbana? Victoria's Secret?" She sliced through a radish. "Come with me in the morning. We'll use my discount. We got some famous purses too."

Three days later Lupe spent the afternoon at a beauty salon in the barrio: pedicure, manicure, hair shampooed and uneven ends trimmed. At home after a bath she slipped into a summery light blue designer dress, knee length with thin shoulder straps and modest décolletage. She hugged and kissed her mother and son good night.

"Watch out for purse snatchers," Arabela said.

"Say hi to Paco for me," Rodrigo Carlos told her.

Lupe grasped her new black leather purse and began walking toward the subway station. Her new shoes fitted well, complemented purse and belt. A rhinestone barrette gripped her ponytail.

Just before sunset she reached the arch at Plaza de Garibaldi, arriving twenty minutes before their scheduled meeting. But Lupe wouldn't stand near the curb until she judged he would drive up if he appeared punctually. She walked around the vibrant music-rich plaza, looked into the restaurant windows, tried to see beyond cantina doors while enjoying an exploration impossible with her son and unicycle.

Lupe planned to wear her wristwatch newly acquired at a bargain from one of the barrio's leading fences and said to be a Rolex. But she feared that somewhere between home and the subway it would be ripped off her arm, and she changed her mind.

A glance at the wristwatch of a passing musician told Lupe to go to the curb. *He'll probably be late, but I won't be. And will he recognize me without my unicycle and Carlitos?* She suppressed a laugh. *I'm so conspicuous. Don't be late, Francisco Toledo.*

Lupe watched every black Mercedes sedan that slowed down or stopped, tried to mentally put Paco behind the wheel. She repelled several flirtations, including one marriage offer, prepared to ignore the sporty-looking red car, sitting low and exuding power, but it stopped at the curb in front of her. The passenger door opened.

"You look great." Paco leaned across the seat. "Hop in."

The car radio played *Malagueña Salerosa.* Paco, in gray slacks and a long-sleeved white guayabera embroidered in blue, lowered the volume. He sent the car into the traffic flow, drove swiftly around the block, soon reached Avenida Juárez. Shortly after passing Parque Alameda he looped around the monument nicknamed El Caballito and joined the wash of vehicles on Paseo de la Reforma.

"First time I've seen you dressed up."

"First time you've seen me without my unicycle and son."

"What's the name of that movie you're starring in?"

Lupe laughed, realized she had been tense. She relaxed. "I feel like I'm sitting almost on the pavement. What kind of car is this?"

"Lamborghini."

"Did you wreck your Mercedes?"

"No, that's my business car. This one's for socializing. You like?"

"I think so. Don't tell me what you paid for it."

Lupe enjoyed the ride along the wide street adorned by trees and statuary, a view she missed when she and Carlitos with the unicycle rode the subway to Parque Chapultepec. *On this street we'd get killed in the first block. This is fun.* She also thought of times she and her parents, later Lupe and her husband, had ridden city buses to Chapultepec, the vehicles so crowded they couldn't enjoy the view except for the rare times they found a window seat. Lupe wondered if Paco had ever ridden bus or subway.

Paco drove around El Ángel and rolled onto Avenida Insurgentes Sur.

"Where are we heading?"

"What about the San Ángel Inn?"

"Carlitos and I have been there so often already this week. I don't know."

Paco smiled at her, looked at her legs, exposed to midthigh since she sat, returned his attention to the street.

A few minutes later when he parked at the restaurant Paco placed his hands on the top of the steering wheel and looked straight ahead.

Lupe wondered why he didn't speak nor open his door.

Still apparently watching something beyond the hood of the car, Paco broke the silence. "Lupe, you need to know something." He reached under his seat, withdrew a small blocky-looking pistol, and showed it to her. "Someone who doesn't like me might recognize me and look for advantage. It's because I'm known to often carry large amounts of money. It's my business. A lot of it's done by phone or wire, but there are times a personal touch is needed." He pointed to the glove compartment. "There's another pistol in there. A little larger."

"Are you a criminal? My mother told me to ask."

Paco laughed. "Of course not. It's like I said. You know there's a lot of crime in this city. People with money have to protect themselves—sometimes even from cops."

Lupe, determination in her eyes, authority in her tone, twisted to face him better. "I lost Carlitos's father to crime. I don't want to know any more gangsters. But you promised me a meal, and I'm hungry."

Paco smiled. "Then you believe me?"

"We'll see."

He put the pistol beneath his shirt and under his waistband against his back, and they went inside.

Paco told Lupe he would properly deliver her to her home or she would have to take one of his pistols. Therefore, despite Lupe's admonition that hostility would likely welcome Paco and his Lamborghini, he drove Lupe through the mostly dark Barrio de Tepito and to her front door.

"I hadn't imagined such a meal," Lupe told her mother. "Hors d'oeuvres I'd never heard of. Enough salad to choke a rabbit. And a juicy thick steak. Cut it with a fork."

"No champagne?" Arabela's bedroom light had come on before the sound of Paco's departing vehicle faded. In her nightgown she sat with Lupe in the kitchen.

"He offered, but I asked for red wine. 'Imported from France,' the label said."

"Did he drink a lot?"

"One Chivas Regal with ice and water and a glass of wine like mine." She told her mother about Paco's pistols, repeated his explanation.

"Do you believe him?"

"I think so. It makes sense. How did Carlitos do?"

"Just fine. Except the TV acted up during *Sábado Gigante,* so we turned it off and went to bed early. Go to Mass with us in the morning?"

"Yes. Mama, Paco asked me to go out again next Saturday. I told him Carlitos and I will meet him today by the kiosk at Plaza Garibaldi and I'd let him know."

"Think you'll say yes?"

"We'll see. I kissed him good night, just briefly."

"You don't want to get hurt again."

"No, Mama. I surely don't."

Lupe went with him. After her usual warnings about the hazards of the Barrio de Tepito she allowed Paco to pick her up at home, where Lupe introduced him and her mother to one another, and where Carlitos induced him to color an elephant in his coloring book. *If Mama had any doubts about Paco,* Lupe thought as they drove off, *he chased them away with that smile and his interest in my son. Now if I can just get rid of my own doubts . . .*

Paco took her to the Thoroughbred races at Hipódromo

de Las Américas, where they sat in the Turf Club, enjoyed snacks and drinks at the table in Paco's box, and bet on nearly every race. She had never been to the races.

When the Turf Club manager stopped by to chat he congratulated Paco on his companion and complimented Lupe on her coiffure and her white sheath dress.

"He called you Johnnie," Lupe said when the manager left.

"My name is Juan Francisco. Mostly I'm Paco, but some friends call me Juan, and others have anglicized it to Johnnie. They joke that I'm a gringo because of being born in the United States."

Two other men stopped to talk, called him Johnnie. "They just wanted a good look at you," Paco said.

He drove to a restaurant in Coyoacán.

The only wagers Lupe won had been when, instead of making choices based on the horse's name or the color of the jockey's silks, she copied Paco's bets.

"What a wonderful day, Mama. Paco financed me, and I won what Carlitos and I earn in a week on the unicycle. And those jockeys—they could ride in the circus."

"Did Paco shoot anyone?"

"Oh, Mama. No one tried to rob him."

"I suppose you'll see him again?"

"So far, so good. But he's going on a business trip to Chihuahua. He'll look me up when he gets back in a week or two. Mama, Paco wants to take me to Cuernavaca."

"That's an easy day trip."

"He means for the weekend."

She packed the blue dress with designer jeans and Nike sneakers and wore a red dress by Armani. *Finally, living in*

Tepito has become a blessing. In Cuernavaca she let Paco pose her for photos outside the cathedral; at several locations inside the Jardín de Borda; inside and outside the Palacio de Cortés, where she stood beside Diego Rivera's life-size painting of Emiliano Zapata with his white horse, As de Oro; and in front of the equestrian statue of Zapata in the main square. Throughout, she wished her son were enjoying the same attractions.

Now they sipped *horchata* in the shade of a refreshment stand across the street from the former mansion of Cortés and observed the automobile traffic and the people walking by, and they studied one another.

"You enjoyed modeling for me," Paco said.

"But that's not being a professional. Besides, don't forget my film career." Lupe smiled over the top of her cooling white refreshment.

"You've got the looks, the moves." Paco took her hand and held it. "Guadalupe María Estudillo, I want to marry you. We'll go to Paris on our honeymoon."

"I thought this is our honeymoon."

He released her hand and leaned back. "I mean it. When we return I'll buy us a nice place in Coyoacán or wherever you want. A large house. For your mother and Carlitos too. An army of servants to cook and clean and do laundry. You and your mom can relax all day watching soap operas or sitting in the Jacuzzi. We'll put Carlitos in a private school, later a top university in California or New York. What do you say?"

"I say you sneaked something into your glass."

"I love you, Lupe. You've got to think about it."

Lupe nodded, sipped her refreshment, watched Juan Francisco Toledo. *This kind, smiling man couldn't be a criminal. He just couldn't be.*

They stood at the kitchen sink in midafternoon, Lupe helping her mother prepare the meal while Carlitos kicked a soccer ball in the street with friends a few doors away. Lupe had
talked almost nonstop about Cuernavaca and the drive to
and from that city, especially about the rare unobstructed
views of volcanoes Popocatépetl and Ixtaccíhuatl, and the
attractions of the popular vacation city itself, including the
weather, springtime in midwinter. Lupe felt that Carlitos
had missed Paco more than the boy missed her.

"I liked the food, Mama, but it didn't compare to yours."

"I would think not."

"Paco took lots of photos. When they're developed he'll
show us." Lupe related his marriage proposal, the promise
of a honeymoon in Paris, told of the large home he would
acquire for all of them. "What do you think?"

"He should have stayed to eat with us."

"His car. The neighborhood. I mean about marrying
him, the house."

"I know." Arabela started shaping tortillas from a hill of
dough. "He might be a crook. A bad one. A major criminal."

"But he just couldn't be. Not the way he is. You found
him attractive."

"Yes, and he's convincing," Arabela said.

"Besides—"

"Besides, Lupita, you love him."

Lupe hugged her mother. "I just can't help it."

"We'll keep our fingers crossed."

"And I'll have my hair pinned up tomorrow and a small
boy on my shoulders."

Paco took Lupe to dinner frequently over the next few weeks,
always including her mother and son in the invitation. To
Lupe's pleasure Arabela usually declined for her and the boy,

though when Paco and Lupe headed for another weekend in Cuernavaca, Paco insisted they participate. Arabela and Carlitos joined them.

Lupe wouldn't let him keep her out late except sometimes on a Saturday. "I have a day job, remember."

One night when they sipped wine and listened to a singer at a variety show, Paco told her, "You could be on that stage."

"You mean with my unicycle?"

Paco's out-of-town commitments often kept him away for a week or more.

"I know people," Paco said. "I can get you a phone and we can keep in touch."

"Someone would break in and steal it."

When Lupe questioned him about whom he saw and what he did he smiled and patted her knee. "Just business, Sweetheart, boring business."

Though Paco occasionally named a city where he would be she fretted about his refusal to discuss his work. Still, Lupe felt her love for him expand and deepen.

When Paco said he found the ideal house, however, and urged her to bring Arabela and Carlitos to live there with him, the women balked.

"It's too soon," Lupe told him.

Her mother nodded.

"What are we waiting for?" Paco said.

"I need more time." Lupe touched his hand. "That's all." *I have to be sure of you.*

That night after Carlitos had gone to sleep Lupe and her mother talked.

"You had seemed so certain about him," Arabela said.

"Yes. And I love him and want the things we've talked about. It's also a way out of the barrio for all of us." She looked at her hands folded together on the kitchen table in front of her. "But these out-of-town trips, his reluctance to talk about them . . . "

Lupe and Carlitos continued their routine with the unicycle, returned home before dark every day with flirtatious marriage proposals for Lupe and their pockets tight with coins. She thought about Paco all day, yearned for him when he took one of his trips, liked it when he began sending her telegrams.

If Paco were gone on Saturday night she missed him more. She walked to Mass on Sundays with her mother and Carlitos and continued to purchase *Excélsior* on the way home so she could read the funnies to her son.

"Mama," she said on this Sunday when they approached their door, "I've decided to marry Paco as soon as he returns from Monterrey. Everything will be all right. You'll see. We'll move into that castle he found, or another if it's no longer available. It will be a new beginning for us."

"I hope so. If he disappoints you I think I'll—"

"He won't. I can feel it."

Carlitos tugged her hand. "Can I have a bicycle? Paco will teach me to ride."

"You bet, Champ. With your sense of balance you'll learn easily."

"And a horse too?"

"We'll have to see about that."

Arabela said, "I won't let any stranger take over the kitchen entirely."

"Of course not, Mama."

While Arabela in the bedroom put their coats and purses away, and Carlitos changed out of his Sunday clothes, Lupe with the newspaper at the kitchen table placed the first section to one side and began hunting for the comic pages. But out of the corner of her eye she caught a headline and photograph on the front page.

The story told how a robber had been shot and killed while leaving a bank in Monterrey. He had long been sought, always eluded arrest. Wearing a rubber mask in the likeness of Porfirio Díaz, he always fled without a trace after exiting one of the two dozen banks authorities accused him of robbing in the last two years.

Lupe sat to continue reading.

"He was the cleverest bandit we ever encountered," a Monterrey police spokesman said, "responsible for numerous robberies, usually in the north. He wore a 'presidential' mask and worked alone. We thought of him as Public Enemy No. l."

The accompanying photograph, grainy and taken from a distance, showed a man in a business suit sprawled on his back outside a bank, his shirt front bloody. A policeman, mask in hand, stood over him.

Lupe squinted to make out the robber's face. *Don't let it be Paco. Please don't.*

She returned to the article.

It identified him as Juan Francisco Toledo, twenty-four years old, from Mexico City.

"We never knew his name before," the police spokesman said. "Authorities all over Mexico referred to him as Johnnie the Gringo."

Lupe's sobs brought her mother and son hurrying to her side.

TALES OF SPAIN

Maimónides

◇◇◇◇◇◇◇◇◇◇◇◇◇◇◇◇◇◇◇

Mike and Valerie had quit the freighter at Barcelona, which they enjoyed for a week. Walking in the tracks of El Cid, they loved Valencia. But they left Ibiza to the partygoers after two days and relished the beach and slow pace of Alicante before abandoning the Mediterranean shore. Now they hoped to obtain a good look at ancient Córdoba on the banks of the Río Guadalquivir.

"This is the hottest damn place I've ever seen." Mike, shirtless and barefoot, sat under a vent for the air-conditioning system. "When Spaniards die the bad ones are probably sent here."

"I'll check my guidebook," Valerie said.

"I'll laugh at that remark next time I have the energy."

"Be sure to wear a hat." Valerie lay in bed in their hotel room, sheet pulled up to her chin, long blonde hair spread over the pillow like the lace fans for sale in the lobby.

Mike moved to the edge of the bed. "You look great with your hair like that. Are you certain you're sick?" He admired the outline of her form and tugged on the sheet.

Valerie tugged back. "Barbarian. Go have your day on the town."

"Maybe I don't want to go." Mike sat beside her.

"You cannot stay here and listen to me retch every hour on the hour."

"I'd better stay in case you need the doctor again."

"I'm kidding. The worst is over."

"It's so hot."

"It's Córdoba in August."

"But you're my guide and interpreter. I won't have anyone to talk to."

"Take the guidebook. It's in English and Spanish. Reading it is like talking. And you'll probably meet some statues. Talk to them."

Mike sighed, started putting on his shoes. "You're getting better."

"I am, Honey. But I want to be alone with my book."

"Must have been the shrimp. Which one are you reading?"

Valerie pointed to it on the nightstand: *The Spirits in Our Midst.*

Mike stepped to the closet. "You just read that."

"This is a different one."

"You don't believe that stuff do you?"

"You never lived around my grandmother and her friends."

"There's your spirits, her creaky old house."

"Nor," Valerie said, "my grandfather and his."

Mike put on a lightweight shirt, sat again to tie his shoes, smiled at her. "I guess I'll have to find a shady place by myself, to eat lunch, by myself."

"And walk around by yourself." She picked up the book and opened it.

"What if I get lost?"

"Ask a Civil Guard for directions. They know everything—and everybody."

Mike picked up his hat and camera, put extra film into his pants pocket. "New in town. Don't know anybody. Don't know the language. Woe is me."

Valerie giggled. They kissed.

"Spirits." He shook his head. "Fortunately you possess other attributes."

"You have permission to withdraw. Please git."

Mike put on his hat, purchased when they arrived the day before, the black, flat-brim, flat-top *sombrero cordobés* with chin strap. "I feel like a tourist."

Valerie laughed and tossed him their guidebook. "Don't forget a bottle of water."

Taking photos frequently, Mike strolled the Roman Bridge, examined the Great Mosque and Royal Stables, and noted the grist mills along the banks of the Guadalquivir. When he passed through a Moorish archway in the historic quarter of Córdoba he discovered a small plaza. It invited him like an oasis to seek relief from the breezeless sky and roasting sun, a quiet park with trees, shrubs, and a few stone benches. *Time for a rest break. Even the birds are in hiding.*

He stepped off the narrow flagstone walk and sat on a bench in the shade of date palms. Mike sipped from his water bottle and set his hat beside him. He opened the guidebook, whose map soon told him he had found Plaza de Tiberíades.

The book identified granite statues there as representations of native sons prominent in Córdoba a millennium apart, Jewish philosopher-doctor-rabbi Maimónides and Roman statesman Séneca. *Good. Your names are familiar. Sorry I missed you boys. Probably would it have been too hot to talk anyway.*

Mike read a few more paragraphs, looked to the far end of the park, and sipped water. The other benches had become occupied. A group of Japanese arrived through the arch, paused for their guide's lecture, and moved on. A guided cluster of Germans followed on their heels. By the time they departed, and Mike looked up, an elderly stranger stood beside him.

"May I share your bench?" the man said. "The others are also taken, and I am a bit weary."

Mike made room. "I'm surprised anyone's out, including me."

"Oh, we get used to it. And most visitors are in a hurry, especially Japanese, Germans, and Americans. So they do not linger, perhaps can ignore the heat."

"But your turban, your robes. Isn't that too much?"

"Young man, my attire works just the opposite."

"I'll take your word for it. Sounds like you live here."

"I was born here, but we moved away when I was little. Now I return regularly."

"Your English is good. Just a slight accent."

"Thank you. I seem to have become a polyglot, having traveled so much." He laughed. "Some think of me as The Wandering Jew."

Mike extended his hand and introduced himself.

The stranger grasped Mike's hand. "Call me Ben. English?"

Cold hand. His attire must work. "American."

"From where?"

"California."

"Oh. The United States. Here it's best to say it. 'America' to us could be Mexico or any one of a dozen other countries."

"Fair enough. Have you been there?"

"Oh no. It's such a long voyage by sea. And I wouldn't want to fly. Besides, my place is here, here and Cairo."

"Why Egypt?"

"I'm quite well liked in Egypt. I raised money, you see, to ransom Egyptian prisoners from the Crusaders in the twelfth century. Later I became leader of the Jewish community in Egypt. I spend a lot of time in Cairo, at the library and around."

Mike lifted an eyebrow, studied him, mentally fitted the

man into a straight jacket. *It's the heat. No sense contradicting him. Should I humor him? And he's pleasant, likable.* Do you have a home here?"

"No, the Berbers took it, part of the Almorávides Empire. Terrible times for Jews, other races. You could convert to Muslim, be killed, or leave. We chose exile and lived all over southern Spain for years. I am also familiar with the Holy Land and Morocco, Alexandria, other places."

"I see. So you have friends here? Lodge in a hotel?"

"I do not know many people nowadays. As I said, I move around a lot."

Mike considered excusing himself and continuing his self-guided tour. *But it's too hot. 'Twelfth century'?* He sipped water, proffered the bottle to Ben, who refused it.

"I am talking too much," Ben said. "One of my vices. Tell me about yourself, lad. Where do you live in your part of America? What is your profession?"

"We're in a little town on the Mexican border, San Diego. As for a profession, I plan to write, but I just graduated in literature and history, so it's going to be 'student' for a while longer, graduate school so I can get a good job someday."

"Good luck to you. I do a little writing myself. Did you study any philosophy?"

"No. My wife has."

"She may have heard of me. You see, I became the first to write a systematic code of all Jewish law, a lengthy, difficult task." Ben waggled his head. "And I have what might be called lesser works. Let's see:

"Astrology: It does not merit being called a science. After all, Man cannot be expected to be dependent on the constellations. That's folly. Resurrection: I usually write about immortality of the soul, not the revivification of dead bodies. That gets me in trouble with some Jews." He laughed. "They still attempt to figure out what I believe."

Mike again considered leaving. *Valerie should hear this nut's comments.*

"And," Ben continued, "there have been—" He greeted a passerby in robe and sandals. "Lucio. Good morning to you. Join us."

"I cannot, Rambam. I must reach the market before this day becomes hot." He nodded, first to Ben, then to Mike, and left under the arch.

You mean it's not already hot? "What did he call you?"

"Rambam. Rabbi. I am also a medical doctor."

Humor him. "You must keep busy."

"Our people need so much. Sometimes I feel like I'm working myself to death. I'm nearly seventy, and I must meet patients this afternoon in Cairo." Ben gestured, indicating the entire little park. "I hope I'll be buried in a pleasant garden like this." He stood. "Again I jabber like a happy sparrow. Forgive me. Come. You might want to photograph my monument."

His monument? Mike put on his hat and followed Ben to a life-size stone carving nearby of a man seated on a blocky pedestal close to the arch.

"What do you think, young man?"

Mike read the inscription:

"Moisés Ben Maimón (Maimónides) 1135-1204"

"Nice work." Mike looked at the old-timer beside him. *But wait: The same turban, the robes, the sandals. Even the face. Trims his beard identically. All he needs is a book like this statue has.* "May I photograph you beside the monument?"

"I would be pleased." Ben stood close to the likeness of Maimónides.

"My wife will like this," Mike said. "I'm sure she's studied Maimónides." He photographed them from various angles, also made close-ups of each face.

"I ask strangers to call me Ben because it is simpler. They often do not believe that I am actually Maimónides."

"No, Ben, I guess not." *But what a marvelous imperson-ation. I suppose he'll ask for a donation. If he does I'll give him a few pesetas.*

"But you, my young friend, I sense something about you, empathy, perhaps something from your past. I wanted you to know."

"Thank you. You animated my day despite the oppres-sive heat." He removed his camera from around his neck.

"Well, then, I'll be off for Cairo."

They shook hands.

Such a cold grip in this heat. Maybe I should get some of those robes. Mike watched him walk toward the arch. But instead of passing under it Ben walked through the adjacent stone wall and disappeared. Mike struggled to not drop his camera.

"Scare you did it?"

"I think that's the word." Mike turned to address a man who had approached from the opposite direction: elderly, khaki shirt, military-style khaki pants, shiny brown boots, pith helmet, cane in one hand, leash of a panting black dachshund in the other. *Englishman. Must live here. They're all over.*

"Ben does that to people. I'm Stuyvesant Denis, colonel, ex-Coldstream Guards."

"He claims that's his statue." Mike introduced himself, nodded toward the monument. "Told me he's Maimónides."

"Quite right, old chap."

"Did you see him go through that wall?"

"Oh, yes. We're accustomed to him."

This one's right out of Hollywood. Central Casting. Just needs a monocle. Gotta get out of here. Heat's getting me. "I need to photograph that statue at the other end." Mike took a few steps in that direction.

"We'll accompany you if you don't mind." The colonel tugged his dog's leash. "Come along, Rommel."

They neared the statue, another stone-carved bearded man in robes, this one hatless, standing on a short pedestal. Mike read the inscription:

"Lucio Anneo Séneca 4-65"

"Roman statesman," the colonel said. "Nero made him commit suicide. Thought Séneca joined a plot to kill him." He cleared his throat. "Sorry. You probably know all this. But I've been here so long I feel like a guide. Lonely, I suppose. Forgive me."

"No problem. All this is new to me. His face certainly is familiar."

"Books perhaps?"

"Maybe, but more recently."

Colonel Denis looked past Mike to a man approaching. "Hello, Lucio. This visitor and I are admiring your statue."

Lucio stopped, shifted his bag of fruit. "Everything good had just about been sold. Yes, my statue, so they say. I will never believe I look like that. How about some dates?" He proffered a sack.

The colonel and Mike took one date each.

And Mike studied the man the colonel had called Lucio. Next he studied the statue: same robes, sandals, short beard. And the name, Lucio. "May I photograph you?"

"Yes. Put me with that libelous statue. You will clearly see it is not I."

Mike hung his camera around his neck, clearly saw the faces were identical. When he finished and thanked him, the man excused himself and started toward the arch at that end of Plaza de Tiberíades. *My camera's safe around my neck this time. But if he walks through the wall I hope I don't wet my pants.*

Lucio, still on the flagstone walk, passed under the arch.

I suppose his bag of fruit wouldn't have survived going through the wall. "Colonel, I better get back to the hotel. Thanks for the tour."

"Quite all right, old boy. I'll be off too. By the way, Talmudic scholars and prestigious Latinists have interviewed those two. Such experts call them spirits."

Mike studied him. *Valerie would feel at home with this bunch.*

"Those two are who they say they are," Colonel Denis continued, "because no one has proved them wrong. So don't let Ben and Lucio disturb you. They're just like you and me, really."

Mike nodded. *I don't think so, really.* He watched Colonel Denis and Rommel depart. He held his breath. They passed under the arch. Mike exhaled.

"Hi, Honey." Valerie, barefoot in shorts and blouse, her hair in a ponytail, sat propped up with pillows on the bed. She held her book about spirits. "You're back early."

"The heat. But I had a fascinating time, uh, intriguing. How's your book?"

"Wonderful. You just have to read a few pages and you'll be a believer."

Mike didn't respond, placed his hat and camera on a chair, and sat on the edge of the bed. "You look well again."

"I'm fine. Tell me about your day."

He removed his shoes. "You'll be surprised—or probably not." He suppressed a smile. "You see, I had sat on a bench in the shade at this little park . . . Valerie, I'd like to take a look at your book about spirits."

THE OLD KINGS

"Come in, everybody. Enjoy this rarest corner of the wonderful cathedral of Toledo. Through here, everybody. It's a marvel. You will be surprised. Yes, the old kings live."

He radiated honesty and humility, and unlike many of the docents he kept his spiel short and sincere. When visitors accepted his request and entered the chapel they usually liked his brief lecture, appreciated the details presented by this slim elderly man wearing a black suit with black beret and neatly knotted black tie. They heard history unknown to most of them, regularly left coins in his cigar box on the stone bench near the entry.

"The Visigoths began to oust the Vandals from Spain in the year 412," Atanasio Agramonte told them. And he would move back a few steps, motioning them to follow. "The Visigoth King Eurico completed that conquest of the Vandals and became the first independent king of Spain. Eurico ruled from 466 to 484. We haven't found his remains but we're certain he is buried right here." And Atanasio would take another step back and gesture to a large marble flagstone in the chapel floor.

"We think that's true because ancient Spain constructed this chapel over the ruins of the royal cemetery of the Visigoths, and Toledo had been their capital. However, we

did find the bones of Recaredo I, brother of San Hermenegildo. By the way, Recaredo became a good Catholic." Atanasio would remove his beret, step to one side, and point to
another large marble flagstone.

After a pause he returned his beret to his head. "And we
located the tomb of the last Visigoth king, Rodrigo. He's the
one the Arabs defeated at Medina Sidonia in 711. That battle established Moorish rule and drove the Visigoths out."
Atanasio pointed to another flagstone in the floor.

This had been Atanasio's routine from the beginning,
and he felt comfortable, helpful. But ever since a Civil
Guard took up a post one day in the adjacent Chapel of San
Juan, Atanasio had become uneasy in what he thought of as
his domain, the Chapel of the Old Kings. For none of the
other docents had ever claimed this chapel or led a group
there for even a brief visit. Atanasio didn't understand why
they hadn't, but he felt glad for it.

Perhaps the regular docents aren't supposed to, he thought.
*Maybe they don't know history the way I do. I'll wager they
haven't even learned, as I have, about Spain's formidable treasure of silver and gold stored next door in the San Juan Chapel.*

He also didn't understand about that watchman from
the dreaded Civil Guard. Why now and not previously?
Had there been reports of evildoers learning about the gold
and silver? Whatever the reason, the guard made Atanasio
uneasy. *Is the Generalissimo pursuing me?*

So when that stoic sentinel in his three-cornered black
hat of patent-leather stood near the front of the adjacent
chapel and seemed to be listening, Atanasio talked softer
and faster. When Atanasio lacked customers, as he thought
of the visitors, he sat on the stone bench and read the *ABC*
or pretended to doze.

A Spanish erudite once said that if someone had only one
day to see Spain, that person should spend it in Toledo. The

learned man's reasoning: Toledo is the best example of the genuine Spanish land, civilization, and history.

Atanasio felt the same way about the stony little city virtually unchanged since medieval times. Before becoming a docent in the cathedral he had often visited Toledo with his wife and children. After their sons and daughters married, Atanasio and Beatriz continued visiting at least once a year, staying in a pension close to El Greco's former home.

They often walked to the Alcántara Bridge and stared down at the Río Tajo in its lazy loop around most of the city. Sometimes they would cross the San Martín Bridge and walk to the Roman ruins, for Beatriz relished history almost as much as Atanasio did.

Since Beatriz's death he had visited alone, while lodging in the same place, continued to stroll across the Alcántara Bridge and the San Martín, and often reviewed the Roman ruins.

And he suffered, for Atanasio missed the companionship of his wife and family. He preferred not to move from Madrid, for he cherished his good fortune to have been born there and not in Catalonia, for instance, or the Basque country or Extremadura. Andalucía would have been a decent birthplace, though he didn't like the accent of native Andalucíans.

But he felt the need for a permanent change of domicile. And Toledo lured him. He explained his plan to his youngest son, an attorney, the premiere thinker among the siblings.

"But Toledo is so small," the son, Agustín Roberto Agramonte, complained.

"Yes. My retirement check will go further there."

"That's another thing: You should have applied long ago for an army pension."

"I wouldn't have gotten it. I fought on the losing side, remember."

"You should have tried. And you should have taught at a government school."

"I will always refuse to have anything to do with the Generalissimo's government."

"Father, you've made your existence more difficult."

"But not beholden to *that man*."

"There's nothing to do in Toledo."

"There used to be. And Toledo's history lives. That's enough for me."

"It's so quiet there," Agustín Roberto said.

"Exactly. The Generalissimo and his Civil Guard won't be so ubiquitous. I'll be able to enjoy more vivid thoughts about your mother, all of you."

Agustín Roberto reached for his wine. He sipped, and to better look through the vast window he adjusted his position on the rattan couch in his living room high above central Madrid. His view included the glass-and-steel skyscraper across the Gran Vía from the similar building he lived in. When he turned back he set the wine on the glass coffee table. "Father, this is your home, always has been."

Atanasio looked through the window at the nearby skyscraper. But his thoughts moved to how he and other defenders of the Republic had held Madrid against the Arabs and other troops of the Generalissimo, how they wept when the Republic surrendered, but how proud they felt that Madrid had not fallen. Atanasio pitched his rifle into a ditch and walked across Madrid to his parents' home. Now he shook his head. "Yes, but it's not my home anymore."

"But we can look after you better here."

"I'm not that old, maybe never will be."

Agustín Roberto opened a silver box on the coffee table, removed a small cigar, offered one to his father, who shook his head, and took one for himself. "I just don't understand."

"Not one building like this has constructed itself in Toledo." Atanasio pointed to the floor. "I can easily walk all through or even around Toledo in one day. I feel like a knight of old when I stroll those ancient streets of stone."

When Atanasio moved permanently to the pension near El Greco's former home he soon realized that, whether or not he earned money, he needed something to do besides walk and think and reminisce. And when he recalled that the Chapel of the Old Kings lacked plaques, docent, and visitors, he set his mind to establishing himself there.

He already knew enough English from self-study to defend himself before the hordes of British tourists Spain attracted. In self-exile he had learned a lot of French during three years of toil in the vineyards of Burgundy following the war. And his lengthy experience teaching history at a private school in Madrid would help him to fit in.

Those Spaniards who call themselves Catalonians or Basques will just have to speak Castilian if they want to learn anything from me. I can do this. I've seen the statues of the Visigoth Kings outside the Palacio Real in Madrid. Their period is long neglected and seldom discussed. Yet facts about them abound, apocrypha too.

On the morning of the first day at his new job Atanasio had felt twenty years younger. In the mirror watching himself shave he talked to Beatriz and he mentally practiced his spiel on her. He enjoyed the feel of his new white shirt, took a long time knotting his tie just right, liked the fit of his newly brushed black suit and the angle of his beret.

The early morning walk to the cathedral had never been more pleasant.

And from the start, Atanasio enjoyed the attention he drew from visitors he attracted to the chapel. Even those who had never heard about the Visigoth kings paid close attention, made him feel important, wanted. He almost considered it camaraderie.

His love of the history and proximity to it in *his* chapel soon led him to expand his stories about some of the old kings. After all, Spain should be ashamed that all the Visigoth kings were not buried there, that many lay in unmarked, undiscovered graves. So with enough facts and a modicum of imagination to enliven the long-ago monarchs, Atanasio told about them anyway.

"This way, everyone. The old kings live. Leovigildo, the strong . . . Recesvinto, who wenched . . . Ervigio. who made his own wine . . . Wamba . . ."

The coins dropped into his cigar box jangled in his pants pocket on the way home, and they encouraged Atanasio to splurge from time to time: a magazine, a cigar, a shoe shine, a meal away from the pension.

And he realized that while he still missed Beatriz the stabs of loss and loneliness had diminished in number and intensity, his new toil infused him so. *This work is what I needed. I want to do this for the rest of my life.*

With the first chill of fall, tourism diminished, and the squirrels grew busier around the oak trees. By midwinter the number of visitors dropped additionally, but most who showed up were Spaniards, so his Castilian flowed almost continually.

Atanasio felt good, happy.

Only the stationing of the Civil Guard in the unvisited niche next door darkened Atanasio's reign in the Chapel of the Old Kings.

One cold day toward the end of that same winter Atanasio noticed a well-dressed man talking softly to the Civil Guard at the entrance to the Chapel of San Juan. Atanasio stepped to his bench and sat, holding his *ABC* in front of his face.

When he lowered it he caught the well-dressed man nodding toward him. The guard also looked and nodded. Atanasio tensed, remained so the rest of the day and all along his walk to the pension, where he tried to relax with a small glass of Manzanilla.

On the following day one of Atanasio's first visitors asked so many questions that Atanasio began to perspire despite the cold. "What's this about Recaredo?" and "You say Wamba lost his left hand in a sword fight?"

This man likes his history too. But there is something about his expression, his tone.

As soon as Atanasio returned to the pension he reached for the Manzanilla.

The next morning Atanasio had just set his cigar box open on the bench and adjusted his beret when a stern-faced older man, gray, robust, arrived asking questions.

"Since early last summer," Atanasio replied.

"Oh, yes," he answered to another query. "Hired by the bishop, historical monuments sector." *Just a little fib. What harm can it do?*

And the stern-faced man continued with his interrogation.

Atanasio feared that the man held a top position with the Civil Guard. *The Generalissimo is after me for sure. I wish he would hurry up and die.* Atanasio, flustered and embarrassed and now also afraid, decided to leave.

He excused himself, picked up his cigar box, closed the lid, and clasped the box to his chest.

The stern-faced man turned toward the passageway and motioned.

Two armed men in uniform, each topped by a three-cornered black hat of patent-leather, stepped into the Chapel of the Old Kings and led Atanasio away.

THE COUNT
OF BARCELONA

◇◇◇◇◇◇◇◇◇◇◇◇◇◇◇◇◇◇◇◇◇◇◇◇◇

Hamilcar Acosta had just settled onto his three-legged stool beside his box of shoe-shine paraphernalia when he saw the birds, a dove and a hawk. They rode in a small wooden cage a boy toted in the usual river of men, women, and children flowing in both directions along the wide promenade, some hurrying, others strolling.

Twice he watched the boy approach adults, a nicely dressed young woman, then a man, to offer them better looks at his passengers, perhaps trying to sell the birds. Hamilcar saw the woman exchange comments with the boy, smile, shake her head, and slowly move away. The man slowed down, glanced at the birds, frowned, and resumed his quick pace.

Hamilcar looked around for potential customers of his own, motioned for men to step close, seldom drew even a glance, and watched them walk away.

And the boy with his caged dove and hawk arrived in front of him.

"Buy some birds, Count?"

"How do you know I'm called that?"

"I'm on Las Ramblas a lot, so I know. Everybody knows you."

"I see. What would I do with two birds?"

"You could teach them tricks. Charge people to watch."

"I don't think so, though I would prefer it to shining shoes. What's your name?"

"Sixto." He wore black cotton pants too small, a much-washed dingy-white T-shirt, a faded red bill cap, and sandals gray with age, cracked and peeling. Undomesticated reddish-brown hair escaped beneath his cap.

"How do such unmatched creatures wind up in your portable jail?"

"The dove is sort of a pet. She hung around our yard. So I just picked her up and put her in so a neighbor's cat wouldn't get her."

"How do you know she's female?"

"She's so pretty, delicate."

"Doves are always in pairs."

"I've heard that, Maestro. Not this time."

"Uh-huh. Tell me something, Sixto. Why hasn't the hawk gobbled her up?"

The boy raised the cage to see through the slats. "Why would he do that?"

"Hawks do things like that. It's their nature."

"He looked sick." Sixto nodded at the larger bird. "One day he walked around the yard a lot and sat down. I thought a dog or the neighbor's cat might get him too, so I put him in with the dove. He's feeling better now."

"How do you know the hawk is a male?"

"The way he looks at the dove. He's very protective."

Hamilcar nodded, studied the birds, the boy. "How old are you?"

"Fif—thirteen." And Sixto told him more, how he lived with his mother, a widow who took in sewing and often cooked in a small restaurant near their apartment. "She gets angry when I skip school to do odd jobs or run errands. She says I should study so I can become a doctor or lawyer, but I'm going to be a businessman."

"Your mother is wise. Do what she says. How long have you tried to sell them?"

"Three days. I have to take them home now and see if there is anything for them to eat. Buy them, Count."

"I don't know. They don't sing."

"Think of the money you'll make after you teach them tricks. Meanwhile you can talk to them. And they don't talk back." He smiled.

How does this boy know I'm lonely? He studied Sixto, the much-washed shirt and too-small pants, the disintegrating sandals. *I can't even trade him a shine for the birds, not with that footwear.*

"You'll grow to love them, Count."

Hamilcar continued to vacillate. *It's easier for me to get shoe-shine customers than for him to sell those birds. And if I can teach them tricks . . . My knee hurts so much when I bend or kneel. It would be one grand day for me if I could quit shining shoes.* He nodded. "How much?"

"Whatever you say, Maestro."

"That's no way to do business, boy."

"I am not much of a businessman yet."

"Neither am I."

Hamilcar watched Sixto examine the box containing the polish and rags and brushes, a shoe's outline on top, where a customer can prop his foot. The boy looked up and smiled. "That's obvious."

Hamilcar stood, elderly, tall in a good-fitting gray suit with black tie, black felt fedora on his head. "You know what I think? I think you stole those birds."

"No, sir. I steal mainly food from neighborhood grocers and trinkets to sell."

Hamilcar smiled, withdrew several coins from his pants pocket, handing them to Sixto. "That's all I have on me."

Sixto accepted the coins. "You are more than fair, Count."

"I still have my pride."

"Everyone knows that. It's why you're called Count. And how you dress, the way you move and talk. Do you want me to carry the birds home for you?"

"It's all right. Please set them on the walk." Hamilcar expected the boy to leave. But Sixto stayed, studied Hamilcar, finally spoke. "You fought in the war."

"Who didn't, in those times."

"With the Army of the East. My grandfather told me." Hamilcar nodded.

"You got wounded several times."

"A common occurrence."

"You won lots of medals."

"A few, all worthless in a box."

"People say that long before the war, in the time of Alfonso XIII, you held a royal title, that you were at least a count."

"People talk too much. And let's not forget which side won, and that tonight's talk often fills the ears of the Caudillo by breakfast."

"My grandfather says the Caudillo's ears should be worn out after thirty years." Sixto turned to leave, turned back. "I've wanted to meet you for a long time."

"Because of your grandfather?"

"And what I hear on Las Ramblas."

"Why didn't you?"

"You looked so stern, I felt afraid."

"I'm not stern. I'm old. Now I think I'll quit for the day."

"Which way do you go?"

"I'm surprised you don't know." Hamilcar motioned to the north.

Sixto laughed. "I hope you'll like the birds."

"We'll see."

"You'll want to name them. I never did."

"We'll see about that too."

Hamilcar Acosta had been a wealthy fifty-year-old planter overseeing fields of grapes and vegetables when the Caudillo led his hordes of Moroccans and other rebelling army units across the Mediterranean to overthrow the Republic. When the fighting ended three years later Hamilcar had lost everything except his life and his wife.

He became a sharecropper. His wife took in washing and sewing. But the shrapnel near his right knee shouted at Hamilcar more each year. When his wife died he moved to Barcelona and set himself up shining shoes near the southern end of Las Ramblas, that busy overwide tree-lined walkway several blocks long that lures and pleases Catalonians and visitors.

Among the plane trees and acacias bordering the walk, vendors line up. They offer snacks and sweets and flowers, soft drinks and newspapers and magazines. And birds in cages: mockingbirds, finches, canaries, parakeets and cardinals and parrots.

Hamilcar glanced at the sun, low, already coloring the clouds. He picked up his shoe-shine box by its strap and hung it over his shoulder, lifted his three-legged stool with one hand, and with the other grabbed the birdcage, poorly constructed with wooden strips of various widths. *The boy must have made this cage because he would have stolen a better one. So maybe he told the truth about not stealing the birds.*

"Let's go home, children." He started walking, examined his acquisitions, and smiled. The dove, white even in the beak, looked feminine. The hawk seemed protective. "Sixto is right. And I've already started talking to you."

Hamilcar walked up Las Ramblas, maneuvered through the crowds in Plaza de Cataluña, and crossed Avenida José Antonio Primo de Rivera to enter his small apartment behind a fruit stand.

"There you go, children." He set the birds on his table. "Rest now and be quiet while I fix our supper." He laughed at himself though he enjoyed the birds' company. "But can you bring me enough coins that I can quit my dreaded shoe-shine business? Let us hope so, for it hurts my pride and my leg."

He carefully opened the cage door on its leather hinges and inserted a cup of water. Next he diced a small pear and half a banana into a pan and gave it to the birds. The dove daintily ate. The hawk snubbed the food. "Not hungry? Tomorrow I'll get you fish and seeds. We'll see." Hamilcar's meal became one he enjoyed regularly: bread and cheese, wine and fried anchovies, olive oil to dip the bread into, a few black olives.

Hamilcar left the birds at home the next day while he tried to figure out how to earn money with them. And he purchased several ounces of beef and diced it for the hawk. On the day after that he fashioned long leather leashes with a slip-knot loop on one end of each. He fettered a bird to each leash and set them on his shoulders, where to his surprise they sat quietly. *They're pets. Sixto stole them.* He placed them into their cage for carrying to his usual spot on Las Ramblas, on the way naming the dove Consentida, the hawk Duque.

At the busy promenade he tied them to a limb on the acacia near him and let them stretch and flap and waddle around. Occasionally one, sometimes both simultaneously, descended to the walkway and strolled around. Consentida cooed. Duque looked stoic.

A man occasionally stopped for a shine. Men and women and children slowed when they saw the birds, sometimes asked questions, usually the birds' names, and Hamilcar enjoyed informing them.

In midafternoon a couple Hamilcar judged to be English stopped and examined the birds. In Spanish the woman asked their names. Then in English she told the man the dove's name meant "Sweetheart" and the hawk's "Duke."

Late in the day a young boy with his parents passed close. The boy, finishing an orange, looked up at the birds on the lower tree branch. He made a harsh sound and hurled a piece of orange peel at them.

Hamilcar started to object but watched with surprise and pleasure when the peel reached its apex without striking either bird. Consentida flew off the limb, caught the peel in her beak, and brought it to Hamilcar's shoulder, from where she dropped it as though in disgust.

"Good girl," he told her. "Let's try that again." From his shoe-shine box Hamilcar retrieved a half-roll left from his lunch and put it into his coat pocket. With Consentida resting on his shoulder, he waited for a gap in the herd of pedestrians, stepped into an opening, and threw a small piece of the roll a short distance into the air.

Consentida flew after it, caught it in her beak in its descent to the sidewalk, and returned to Hamilcar's shoulder. Several passersby applauded.

I'll make her a longer leash, throw the food farther, higher. Yes. This might work.

In his apartment that night after supper Hamilcar made longer leashes for the birds and a T-shaped stand for them to rest on. He also painted a sign with their names and attached it to the stand. And below that he hung a tin cup.

Consentida demonstrated her new trick on Las Ramblas, and the tin cup occasionally resonated with a few coins. Duque looked savage even when Hamilcar fed him a tidbit of meat. But crowds on the picturesque thoroughfare impeded the dove's performances. And Hamilcar often had to attend to a shoe-shine customer.

One afternoon, however, the person who paused before him was neither customer nor someone who would donate coins to watch Consentida fly. He carried a small monkey in a cage.

"What brings you to my palace, Sixto?"

"I wanted to see how you're doing."

"Shouldn't you be in school?"

Sixto smiled. A blue polo shirt, apparently new, had replaced his dingy white T-shirt. Gray denim pants fitted well, and now he covered his auburn hair with a black beret. Tennis shoes had replaced sandals. "I've been watching. You haven't taught the hawk anything."

"I pay him to look scary when little kids approach."

"Meanwhile you still shine shoes."

"I still like to eat. So do these birds you talked me into purchasing."

"You could do better somewhere else, Count. Remember your royal past."

"So now you are my business adviser. What are your plans for that gorilla?"

"Sell him. Or eat him." Sixto laughed. "Look, Count, here most of the people are residents in a hurry to get some tapas or go to work or just wanting fresh air on a break. These birds aren't much of a novelty with so many others caged nearby." He named several locations he said could result in more coins for the tin cup. "In those places most people will be sightseeing, French or English or German, even Americans nowadays."

"But they won't be much interested in shoe-shines like the businessmen who are my customers here."

"At first your shoe-shine business will suffer. But you'll soon make up for the loss, probably even prosper."

"I see. I make you a deal, my wise young friend. If I take the birds to the places you recommend will you attend school regularly?"

Sixto smiled. "Maybe."

The next day Hamilcar filled a small plastic bag with pieces of fish and of pears and bananas. He placed it into his box with the shoe-shine paraphernalia, hung the box over his shoulder. Hamilcar grabbed the birds' stand and his stool. Consentida cooed. Duque frowned.

First he tested business on the Paseo de Colón where Las Ramblas ends near the Columbus statue. Consentida performed well, always capturing the morsel he tossed and returning to the stand with a look of pleasure and coquetry. During an absence of observers he let Duque see a piece of fish. Then he tossed it into the air. Duque's leash reached far enough, but the hawk didn't start swift and agilely like the dove. The morsel fell onto the flagstones. Duque swooped low and grabbed it with his talons. When Hamilcar tugged on his leash Duque flew to the T-shaped stand.

After a few days Hamilcar moved his enterprise to the cathedral, then a few blocks away to the Parque de la Ciudadela, later to the Museo de Arte Moderno. He eventually set up in front of the Iglesia de La Sagrada Familia, where he felt especially comfortable, for as a child he had picnicked on its grounds with his family. Hamilcar had wondered then, as he did now, if the church would ever be finished.

At each site Consentida performed wonderfully, cooing and looking pleased with herself between stunts.

The spectators also enjoyed seeing the hawk up close. They examined his barbaric beak and ferrous talons, watched those predator eyes. So Duque also produced coins.

Hamilcar's birds attracted so much business that he soon quit bringing his shoe-shine box, though he continued to carry his stool so he could sit to rest his leg.

Sixto had been right in advising me to abandon Las Ramblas. And the best thing is my leg doesn't bother me as much. I can walk farther. My appetite has improved. Thank God. I'll never have to shine shoes again.

He set up outside the bullring on Sundays and, always hoping a riot would not break out, at the soccer stadium on game days, though Sixto had not recommended those sites.

The birds drew minimal interest. When Hamilcar encountered Sixto outside the soccer stadium after a contest one day the boy told him why his tin cup held few coins.

"These spectators here and at the bullring are crazy, fanatical," the boy said. "They just want to shout and wave their arms and defend their viewpoints, both before and after an event. We could have an earthquake and they wouldn't notice."

"I suppose I should have known that. Come on. I'll treat."

They walked to a nearby stand where men stood eating ice cream and arguing about the game. The beer vendor next door had more customers.

"I guess I have to be classified among the fanatics," Sixto said. "You, Count?"

"Before the war. And bullfights in my youth. There were giants in those days."

"So long ago."

"Everything I enjoyed happened long ago, my friend." He mentioned the names he had given the birds. Sixto approved, and Hamilcar could see delight in the boy's face because of the enhanced financial situation Sixto had indirectly brought about for him. "Are you heading home now to study?"

"I'll mingle with the crowd a while. They don't pay much attention to me."

Hamilcar thought that seemed strange. Why not seek company his own age? Then he knew: *Pickpocket* .

A few days later on the grounds of Montjuich Castle, Consentida improved Hamilcar's finances even more. The small white dove captured the bite of pear Hamilcar tossed, and when her momentum carried her to the end of her leash she continued flying north.

"The dove got away," a child shouted.

"It sure did," the woman with him said.

Hamilcar barely heard those and other comments, for he stood stunned on the parapet, Consentida's leash in his hand, and he watched her zigzag flight pattern he knew so well.

"That bird's heading for Montserrat," a man shouted while pointing to the ancient monastery far away on the rocky hill to the north, and he laughed.

Hamilcar felt as though his heart had plummeted to his feet.

But as he watched, Consentida performed one of the aesthetic loops he had so loved to see, and this one brought her racing back to him. She glided to a landing on the T-shaped stand, settling next to Duque. Hamilcar thought the hawk glared at her in reprimand. Consentida cooed.

He drew in her leash, saw how the loop fettering Consentida had widened. He inhaled deeply, exhaled, would fix that at home. *But why? The free-flight exhibition looked so much more exciting than the dove's operating from the end of a leash. I could pitch her food higher and farther. We'll do it. Thank you, Consentida.*

So that became the dove's routine. Hamilcar loved it. Spectators cheered it. The hawk watched protectively.

During the next few weeks Hamilcar again took his birds to tourist attractions, thought of the various stops as his "route," as though he were a bus driver. The tin cup attached to the T-shaped stand near the birds' names continually clattered with coins. Hamilcar had not been so happy since he moved to the city.

Even Consentida's sprinting toward the Parque de la Ciudadela one day did not distress him at first. She had just captured the bite of peach Hamilcar tossed while he stood on the waterfront, and he knew she needed to stretch her wings.

But she kept going, zigging and zagging and occasionally ascending.

"Oh, no," Hamilcar said. "Why is she doing that?"

"She pulled a fast one on you, mister," a man said. His companion laughed.

Finally Hamilcar could no longer see the dove, couldn't tell if she had stopped in a tree, hoped she had turned around to race back flying low.

"That bird's hunting a husband," the man said. Again, his companion laughed.

Duque looked so steadily in the direction of Consentida's flight that Hamilcar wondered if the hawk could still see the dove.

Some spectators placed coins in the cup, glanced at Hamilcar, and walked away along the Paseo de Colón. Hamilcar felt that some of them must know he had lost a friend, and more.

Hamilcar, not wanting to believe what he had seen, stared for a long time in the direction of Consentida's flight. But he couldn't find her, and his eyes teared. He turned to Duque. "You lost a friend too." He moved Duque from the stand to his shoulder, picked up the stand and his stool, and walked slowly along the waterfront. The hawk's talons gripped him through his coat in a fierce manner Hamilcar had never felt.

When Hamilcar stopped to rest, set down the T-stand, and leaned against a piling he saw that Duque continued to look in the direction of Consentida's flight.

"You're a smart buddy," he told the hawk. "She had to go sooner or later, didn't she? I knew it and I didn't face it. But wild creatures cannot be fully trusted. Freedom is in their nature. I just don't know if I'm saddened because she took most of my income with her or because harm might come to her."

He studied the hawk for a few moments, watched the sea and nearby freighters, noted the strollers. He nodded at Duque.

"You might as well have your freedom too. Thanks for your help." He removed the leash from the hawk's leg and set him onto the stand. The hawk took a few short steps and stopped to look at Hamilcar.

"Of course. You're hungry." Hamilcar offered several bits of meat to Duque. The bird ate them quickly. Hamilcar reached back into the plastic bag. He found one more bite, studied it a moment, looked at the bird. Hamilcar threw the morsel as high and as far as he could.

Duque flew after it, caught it just before it descended to the walkway, and flew off with it, gaining speed with each flapping of his wings.

Hamilcar watched the hawk diminish in the distance and soon become invisible. "And that's that," he said softly. "I hope you both find mates." He scooped up the coins from the tin cup and pitched the T-stand into the nearest trash container. Head down, Hamilcar slowly started walking home. His leg hurt.

He had almost reached Las Ramblas to begin the northward walk toward the Plaza de Cataluña when a large dark bird startled him by landing on his shoulder. Hamilcar stopped, turned his head. "Is that you, Duque? It surely is. Bless you."

Hamilcar looked more closely. And in the hawk's talons and along the edges of its beak he noticed tiny white feathers and fluffs of down, flecks of blood too.

A week later Hamilcar sat on his three-legged stool next to his box of shoe-shine paraphernalia at the edge of Las

Ramblas and indicated for passersby to have their footwear polished. He had spotted a likely customer to his right and motioned to him when he felt a tap on the back of his left shoulder. He turned. "Hello, Sixto."

"Maestro, how are you?"

"As you see, my friend."

"I heard what happened. I'm sorry."

"How did you obtain such news?"

"Everyone knows the doings of the Count of Barcelona." Sixto had replaced his beret with a well-blocked gray fedora and stood in bright white tennis shoes. He wore short-sleeved blue dress shirt and black cotton pants, both clean and newly ironed. "Did you wring that hawk's neck?"

"I thought about it. He hung around a couple of days but I quit feeding him and he flew away for good. Where are your books?"

"What do you mean, Count?"

"You're supposed to be in class."

Sixto laughed. "This is Sunday."

"Ah, so it is. I like your new hat."

Sixto smiled. "Stole it. The shoes too." He laughed, removed the hat, ran his fingers through his hair.

"Your attire tells me your business improved. How is your mother?"

"Also doing better. Maestro, I'm returning the money you paid me for the birds."

"You're joking. I won't hear of it."

"I'm serious. My pockets are empty just now but I'll have money later."

Hamilcar stood. "Absolutely not. What kind of businessman thinks like that?"

"I expect a big crowd at the soccer game this afternoon."

"One of these days, Sixto—"

The boy laughed.

Hamilcar placed a hand on Sixto's shoulder. "Let's get some ice cream. Someday they'll be calling *you* the Count of Barcelona."

COMPENDIUM

THE WISDOM OF
SANCHO PANZA

◇◇◇◇◇◇◇◇◇◇◇◇◇◇◇◇◇◇◇◇◇◇◇◇◇◇◇◇◇◇◇

Not long ago, one hundred writers from fifty-four countries voted *El Ingenioso Hidalgo Don Quixote de La Mancha*, by Miguel de Cervantes Saavedra (1547-1616), the best fiction in the world.

And as readers laugh and weep with pleasure throughout this masterpiece they soon realize that the misguided old gentleman the story is named for is not the tale's only notable. His sidekick is also sage and philosopher: Sancho Panza.

Readers learn that Sancho is a fat little fellow tall on valor and that he can almost outtalk his chief. They find that Sancho, who loves to drink wine and eat, who adores his wife and village, can endure a lot of punishment, and is alternately as naïve as his donkey and wiser than his boss.

One day near El Prado Museum I browsed at the string of outdoor bookstalls the locals call La Feria del Libro, and I spent a few pesetas. My most-cherished purchase was an outsized 1875 edition of the beloved novel informally referred to as El Quixote. The Biblioteca Universal Ilustrada published my acquisition, which cost me about $6.67 USD. The bookseller promptly showed me an equally huge volume, an 1852 dictionary published by the Real Academia Española.

"You might want this too," he said, "because El Quixote contains so many older words not in today's dictionaries." For the USD equivalent of $7.67 I took it.

Cervantes began what became a two-part masterpiece while imprisoned in Seville, a tax collector accused of mishandling funds. I read it when living nearby in Seville Province at the farm village of Olivares, where I needed that 1852 dictionary and my modern one as well.

Later when I reread the masterwork I took notes about Sancho, who deserves so much credit for the tale's success. The result is what I call *The Wisdom of Sancho Panza*. I hope I do him justice.

Under sponsorship of the wealthy Duke of Béjar, Part 1 of El Quixote was published in Madrid in 1605, Part 2 in 1615, the year before the maestro from Alcalá de Henares died in poverty despite his numerous published novels, plays, and poems.

Nowadays new editions of El Quixote are printed frequently, and the novel can be read in many languages. However, I am privileged and happy to say this translation of selected comments by Sancho is mine.

Don Quixote and Sancho are from a village in Spain's La Mancha, a monotonously flat plain producing wine and grains and dotted by windmills. Cervantes said he didn't want to reveal its location so that all communities of La Mancha would vie for being Don Quixote's village "like the seven cities of Greece contend for Homer."

And that happened.

They also contend for Sancho.

From the story's first clank of armor Sancho immortalizes himself with his advice and pithy commentary. It is Sancho who warns Don Quixote, always seeking "ferocious and perilous battle," not to attack the windmills ("What giants?"

Sancho asks.) . . . not to fight the friars of San Benito, whom Don Quixote believes are enchanters of a princess and that their mules are camels ("This will be worse than the windmills.") . . . and not to unchain the prisoners destined to serve as galley slaves.

Don Quixote frees them anyway and orders them to report to his imagined sweetheart, the beautiful Dulcinea. He directs the slaves to hurry, for the dreaded Santa Hermandad, those omnipotent rural police, will want to recapture the freed prisoners.

That relentless and unforgiving authority will also want to pursue Don Quixote and Sancho because of their good deed. Sancho, who had hidden behind his donkey, convinces his chief that to run would not be cowardice.

"To retire," Sancho insists, "is not to flee."

Many of Sancho's sayings became standard epigrams of the Spanish language, sometimes of the English too:

- "Between the extremes of cowardice and temerity there is valor."
- "Everything that glitters is not gold."
- "A bird in the hand is worth more than a vulture flying."
- "Fortune is a drunken fickle woman."

Long before the end of the tale, Sancho talks like a quite savvy hombre, though Cervantes wrote that Sancho is not bright.

Nowadays Sancho would be called a scene stealer, Mr. Malaprop too, for his misuse of words and imperfect understanding of much of the well-read Don Quixote's vocabulary. Sancho spices the entire story, as sure as his breath smells of garlic. His deeds large and small enliven their days and nights as do his frequently expressed desires to eat and sleep and drink, keep his master out of trouble, obtain a territory to govern, and return to his wife.

Sancho is as integral to the story as are the mishanters

of his tall skinny master, the aging gentleman so determined
to relive the olden days when men were men and valorous
knights roamed from the Round Table to assist widows and
correct injustices, especially those pertaining to lovely damsels.

For the idealistic Don Quixote, of course, one damsel
occupies a golden throne higher than any other woman's.
He built her in his half-made mind, called her the incomparable Dulcinea del Toboso, and ordered his vanquished foes
to report to her and kneel at her feet. Between the two men,
only Sancho saw her as she existed. For his beloved master,
however, Sancho would connive.

The rotund little sidekick and his wife—Cervantes calls
her Juana, then Mari, then Teresa—live at the entry to the
village, where Sancho is a goatherd and Mrs. Panza a farm
wife said to be "around forty." Mrs. Panza is "strong, tough,
robust, dry, and wrinkled, a poor laboring woman, daughter of a farm worker, wife of a roving shield bearer." Their
daughter, Sanchica, is "around fourteen." They also have a
son, but Cervantes leaves him undescribed, unnamed, seldom mentioned. Their village, wherever it might be, is
famed for producing fat acorns.

This, then, is the environment Sancho abandons "without saying good-bye, like a patriarch," when Don Quixote,
promising him a territory to govern, persuades Sancho to
saddle up and ride out with him.

After the ferocious and perilous windmills defeat Don
Quixote, the adventurers converse at length as they ride.
Don Quixote explains additionally about the life of a wandering paladin, and he restricts Sancho to fighting only rab-
ble until becoming a knight. That edict is fine with Sancho,
who sees himself as "peaceful, tame, and calm." His master
grants Sancho permission to complain if he hurts and to eat
when he wants.

"I will guard that precept," Sancho replies, "like a Sunday."

When Don Quixote prepares to enter an ominous forest to investigate a mysterious pounding, he tells Sancho to stand by for three days until he returns.

Sancho, frightened by the loud noise and the dark, asks his master to not leave until dawn, only three hours away.

Don Quixote asks how Sancho knows dawn is so close.

"Fear," Sancho tells him, "has many eyes."

Later, Sancho learns that his leader has seen the long-worshiped Dulcinea "not even four times" and that she is a rustic farm girl named Aldonza Lorenzo, from a village in the province of Toledo. Sancho claims she is tough, can climb the village bell tower and yell to her girlfriends half a league away, and has hair on her chest.

But Don Quixote doesn't accept Sancho's description, instead calmly lists its inaccuracies. The wise little fat man plays along. First, Sancho calls himself an ass for not having recognized Dulcinea's beauty. And in trying to balance that self-inflicted pejorative, he says, "One should not discuss the rope in the house of the hanged man."

Eventually, Don Quixote—by now Sancho has nicknamed him the knight of the sorrowful countenance—decides the time has arrived for him to talk face to face with Dulcinea. But this heretofore indomitable warrior lacks the grit. He wants Sancho to seek her out and obtain permission for the confrontation.

"A good heart," Sancho replies, "overcomes a bad adventure." To this, as is his custom, Sancho adds unrelated comments, including, "Where there is a fence there are not always pigs."

Nevertheless, Sancho pretends to undertake the mission. While he is out of sight waiting for enough time to pass for him to have delivered the message and returned, he talks to himself: "My master, for a thousand signs that I have seen, is crazy enough to be tied up . . . and if the refrain is true that says, 'Tell me the company you keep and I will tell you who you are,' I'm not far behind him, for I'm sillier than he is because I follow and serve him."

Along about then they encounter three farm girls on mules. Sancho decides he will convince Don Quixote that one is Dulcinea and that she is ugly because she has been bewitched, enchanted. The hidalgo falls for this artifice, and Sancho is highly pleased with himself.

A wealthy duke and duchess who give lodging to the wanderers are fascinated by their personalities and deeds. Having nothing else to do, they decide to play games at the visitors' expense. For one, they name Sancho governor of one of their estates, a village of one thousand residents. Sancho reacts with humility but is eager and thrilled.

In the segment concerning Sancho's reign, a humorous anecdote is his settling the squabble between a young woman and a pig farmer. She tells Sancho the farmer attacked her, forcing her to give up what she had guarded "more than twenty-three years," defending it against Moors and Christians, natives and foreigners, tough as an acorn, conserving herself whole, "like the salamander in the fire."

The farmer, however, tells Sancho that while returning home from selling pigs he met her on the trail and ". . . the devil . . . made us yoke ourselves together." He says he paid the woman "sufficiently" but that she demanded more money. They quarreled, he tells Sancho, and she seized him and dragged him before Governor Panza.

Sancho asks if the farmer has any money. He does, twenty *ducados* of silver. Sancho orders him to pay the woman. The farmer complies. She determines that the coins are authentic and leaves happily.

But Sancho immediately orders the surprised farmer to

bring her back, money and all. They soon return, fighting more than the first time.

She demands to know why Sancho sent the farmer to retake the money.

"And did he?" Sancho asks.

In so many words the woman tells Sancho, "Are you kidding?" And she points out, forcefully, picturesquely, that she would die before giving up the silver.

"My sister," Sancho says, "if you had defended your body with the same desire and valor as you have this money, Hercules could not have forced you. Go with God . . . and do not stop within my territory or within six leagues of it in any direction."

He sends the farmer on his way with an admonition. "Be sure to not again get the urge to yoke yourself with anyone."

Sancho becomes a favorite of the duchess, entertaining her with numerous sayings, among them:

- "Unfortunate is the person who by two in the afternoon has not had breakfast."
- "Behind the Cross is the devil."
- "A man who pays his debts is not concerned about having to hock things."

And when asked to accept lashings in order to "disenchant" Dulcinea, whom a conniving Sancho had "enchanted":

- "Every owl to its olive tree" and "A mule loaded with gold climbs the mountain easily."

After Don Quixote tells Sancho to stop presenting his "refrains," the irrepressible Sancho replies:

- "He who cuts the deck does not deal."
- "A dummy at home knows more than a smart man in a strange house."

- "To 'Get out of my house' and 'What are you doing with my wife?' there is nothing to reply."

When a practical joke backfires and Sancho is trampled by "invading troops," he decides he is not a good governor, except of livestock. Sancho calls for wine. Then he goes to his donkey in the stable and embraces him.

"Better to plow," Sancho says, "to dig, to prune, and string the grape vines."

But the duke and his bunch are not finished. Therefore, Sancho undergoes a martyrdom of pinches and pinpricks so that a beautiful local girl, Altisidora, will awake from her deathlike stupor, feigned as a joke on Sancho. Altisidora "revives," thanks Sancho graciously, and says that only love could have deposited the remedy in Sancho's martyrdom.

"It would have been better," Sancho says of the pinches and pinpricks, "if love had deposited it in my donkey."

After several other misadventures they return to their village where Don Quixote, once again a sane Alonso Quijano the Good, soon lies on his deathbed.

Sancho tells him the worst craziness is to die of melancholy instead of being killed, that Don Quixote should leave the bed and take to the trail once more, that surely they would find Dulcinea, disenchanted, lovely, incomparable.

Cervantes died in 1616 at the age of sixty-nine, leaving the legacy of a great and timeless story and a new word to define his hero and similar people, *quixotic*.

The author had set out to so thoroughly spoof the popular romanticized novels of implausible knight errantry that they would expire of their own inanities. And El Quixote accomplished that while gifting to the world two immortal characters who in literature and imagination are still out there, roaming La Mancha.

Don Quixote, riding Rocinante, searches for damsels in distress and injustices to correct.

Sancho, on his donkey, tries to keep his master out of trouble, while making people laugh and showing that a strong heart overcomes bad adventures.

The author has lived in Spain and has spent long periods in Mexico. He lives in his native San Diego.

'Maybe so, Dave, but hardly textbook policing was it?' He looked in the rear view mirror. Gowan shrugged.

Eddie Marriot handed the taxi driver two twenty notes. 'Keep the change.'

'Cheers, mate.'

Marriot took his holdall from the boot of the taxi and walked across the concourse to the entrance foyer of Doncaster Robin Hood Airport. Once inside, he checked his watch, twenty minutes before check-in. He was booked on the 11.30pm flight to Tenerife. Needing to keep a clear head he ordered a coffee from the bar. Sat facing the bar entrance, he consciously looked around. He smiled, so far so good, no activity out of the ordinary by the police or airport security.

Once again he checked his watch, time to move. He pushed the empty coffee mug into the centre of the table and stood up. With his passport and flight ticket in his hand, he reached down and picked up his bag. His heart skipped a couple of beats as he stood in the check-in queue. He passed over his ticket and passport at the desk and checked in his luggage.

'Did you pack your own bag, sir?' The girl working the check-in desk asked.

'Yes,' Marriot replied with a smile.

The girl passed back his passport and ticket. 'Enjoy your holiday.'

'Thanks, I will.'

He was nearly home free. At the security gate, he faced no opposition and sailed through. Things had gone just as he hoped they would. The Monarch Airlines Airbus 320 commenced to taxi. The engine noise increased as the aircraft gathered speed, then the noise abated, with no warning the Airbus slowed. 'Ladies and Gentlemen, due to a technical problem we have to return to the embarkation area,' the pilot said over the aircraft's public address system. The announcement was totally unexpected and Marriot glanced through the aircraft window. A police car escorted by an airport security vehicle was approaching - the game was over.

'So Rab, how are you doing?' Marlowe asked, sitting on the plush Chesterfield sofa in the Bacuss's living room.

'Feeling a lot better than I was a couple of days ago,' the lad replied. He may have felt it, but he didn't look too good from where Marlowe was sitting, two black eyes, a broken nose held together with sticking plasters, and scratches all over his face and hands. He could see Rab's hands trembling as he held his glass. Karen sat next to Rab with her arm around his shoulder. Touching, thought Marlowe, feeling a pang of jealousy, the closeness was something he and Karen had not shared for a long, long time.

'Another drink, Phil?' Charles Bacuss asked. Marlowe held out his glass. It was the best malt whisky he had tasted in a long time. 'So you came through in the end,' he said as he topped up the cut glass tumbler.

'Usually do, sometimes it's not the outcome that we want - but in this case,' he looked to Rab, 'we got the result we wanted. Here's to you,' he held the glass high.

Half an hour later he stood on the Beckside, cigarette in one hand while holding Archie's flex-lead in the other, he thought how different the week from hell could have turned out. He hoped that would be the last he saw or heard from Shag Pile Charlie and his family for a long while. He sat down on a mooring bollard watching Archie rummage in the long grass. Marlowe liked the autumn, the way the wind blew along the Beck and the sound of the water slapping against the *Daisy's* hull. As he sat he shivered, as if someone was walking over his grave. He was oblivious to the fact that at that moment his old friend and former colleague Trevor Cleeves suffered a massive heart attack. He failed to respond to treatment.

END.

'

www.ingramcontent.com/pod-product-compliance
Lightning Source LLC
Chambersburg PA
CBHW020059180626
46812CB00006B/2396